It's Always Story Season

Stories Poems and Essays

An Anthology
By

The Writers Guild
At Bowers House

ISBN 978-1-7947-1411-3

This is a work of fiction. Names, characters, places, and incidents either are the product of the author's imagination or are used fictitiously.

Independently Published by The Writers Guild at Bowers House
Canon, Georgia USA

First Edition November 2021

Illustrations Pixabay

Cover design Charles Prier & Pam Baker

Editing and Publishing Services
By Charles Prier

Know-It-All Publications
1481 Lankford Road
Bowersville, Georgia USA 30516
www.KiaPublications.com

Introduction

By Linda Dye

It came like the night fog coiling and twisting through the cypress knees of the South Georgia swamps, but unlike this eerie fog, it did not dissipate with the morning sun. It put down roots that went deep and reached far, touching the entire world. Its ominous name is Coronavirus.

As privileged, spoiled Americans, we could not perceive being inconvenienced by a lowly virus. There was nothing to fear. We live in the land of technology and medical science noted for miracles. In a few weeks it would be business as usual. The memory of this bug wiped away.

We under estimated our enemy. Covid-19 reared its ugly head and roared back loud and clear. "I will show you what devastation and havoc I can wield."

Thousands died, provisions were in short supply. We covered our faces with masks, stayed six feet apart, washed and sanitized our hands frequently, avoided visits with family and friends, and gatherings of churches, schools, and clubs were suspended.

The Writers Guild struggled, but resolved to continue writing, albeit meetings were halted for many months. Online assignments were completed and submitted via the internet. Stalwart determination overcame the hardships imposed by Covid-19.

Now we have effective vaccines curbing the spread of our nemesis. A few months ago, regular meetings of vaccinated members resumed. Now there is an unimpeded flow of inspiration, fostered by the camaraderie and encouragement of group members coming together. This book, our Sixth Anthology, demonstrates that creative writers cannot be stifled by a Coronavirus pandemic.

Remember… It's Always Story Season. Enjoy!

Table of Contents

Rocky Mountain Christmas

By Pam Baker

The landscape viewed out the train window was fascinating. Ellen couldn't believe the difference in the scenery from day to day. She left the noisy city just one short week ago and had now seen more diversity through her window than she had seen in her whole 19 years. Each day when she woke, it was like she had been transported during the night into a different world. The train passed through large bustling cities and small towns with just a few houses. She saw majestic forests one day and endless miles of treeless plains the next. She rolled over both quiet, winding rivers and the mighty torrent of the Mississippi. One day, she gazed upon acres and acres of cultivated farmland, waiting for spring and strong young farmers to bring forth the corn and wheat from its fields. The next day, she traveled for hours and hours through a sea of prairie grass, seeming to undulate like the waves in the ocean. The flat, empty prairie had now given way to the foothills of the Rockies.

As the train chugged higher and higher, the outside temperature dropped lower and lower. Ellen snuggled under her blanket, her mind going over the enormous changes that had taken place in her life in such a short time. She was enjoying her journey to her new life in the West, but she was tired of traveling and living out of a suitcase. She longed for a proper bed in a real house. But most of all, she longed for her Jimmy. While the rhythmic sound of the wheels and the rocking motion of the train lulled her, Ellen's thoughts drifted back to when she had first met her Jimmy.

Her older brother, Lee, had been working with Jimmy on a neighboring farm the summer of 1860 when Ellen was 15. Lee brought Jimmy home one June afternoon after a hard day's work to collect gear and food so they could go fishing at the pond behind the house. Ellen had been canning tomatoes when the two laughing young men burst into the kitchen. She took one look at the tanned, muscled, blonde boy and was instantly captivated. Jimmy, likewise, was totally enchanted by who Lee called his kid sister. In Jimmy's eyes, she was certainly no kid. While packing a small bag with a couple of sandwiches, a half dozen cookies and two apples, Ellen stole glances at Jimmy. Her cheeks blazed with color when their eyes locked, while Jimmy was caught stealing glances as well. It didn't take long after that before Jimmy found many excuses to accompany Lee home. And it took even less time for Ellen to replace Lee as Jimmy's fishing partner.

That was a magical summer, one Ellen would never forget. The more time they spent together, the more they found to like about each other, and soon they became inseparable.

The following spring, in April of 1861, just when the future looked so promising, their world was turned upside down by the news that Ft. Sumter had been fired upon. Although most young boys and men were reluctant to leave the comforts of home, their girlfriends or wives and children, they all patriotically answered the call to arms. It was what men were expected to do, and they did it. And although Jimmy was not happy about leaving Ellen behind, he too marched off with the rest of the young men, fully expecting to be back home in a few short months–surely it shouldn't take much longer than that.

And now it was October of 1864, over three years later, and there seemed to be no end to the war in sight. The Confederate forces of Jubal Early and the Union men of Phillip Sheridan were facing each other in Virginia's Shenandoah Valley during the Battle of Cedar Creek. When the bloody conflict ended, 2,910 southern and 5,665 northern young men lay dead on the field. Jimmy was among those unfortunate souls.

When Ellen heard the dreadful news, she had been inconsolable. Life seemed to now hold nothing for her but emptiness and she had lain in bed for weeks, unable to face even the most mundane of everyday tasks. During that time, she had concluded that the only way to escape this misery was to truly escape—she would have to start over. She would join the hundreds of others who were journeying out West where a new life awaited. And so, in December of 1864, slightly less than two months after Jimmy's tragic death, Ellen packed all her meager possessions, bid her family a tearful farewell, and boarded this train.

The soothing rocking motion of the train suddenly changed, startling Ellen out of her reverie. The brakes began screaming, and the train began swaying. The back-and-forth motion became so great that the entire train began tipping over, one car at a time. Now completely on its side, the train skidded down an embankment and came to a screeching halt, precariously close to the edge of a cliff. Ellen frantically felt around and located her suitcase, and climbed out the train window, fortunately still clutching the blanket she had recently been so peacefully snuggled under. Standing well away from the train, Ellen looked around her into the eerie silent dark. Then the silence was broken by the train creaking. In seeming slow motion, the locomotive slid over the edge of the cliff. In horror, Ellen watched as the three boxcars, her passenger car, and the caboose were also pulled, one by one, over the side of the mountain.

Ellen suddenly found that she was no longer standing, but lying in a crumpled heap. The shock of the accident had sent adrenaline pumping through her veins, enabling her to escape the wreckage. But now reality had set in and she knew she had not escaped unharmed. Her body ached all over and dark patches of blood soaked her clothing in various places. As her eyes grew accustomed to the dark, Ellen realized no one else was around. She was the only person to escape this horrible catastrophe. The other poor souls on the train must have been severely injured or knocked out when the train toppled over, rendering them unable to escape. She felt enormously grateful that her life was miraculously spared, but now what?

Confused and in too much pain to do much of anything, Ellen dragged herself to some nearby pines to shelter from the cold and wind. She pulled her blanket more closely around her battered and bleeding body and sank to the ground. It wasn't long before she heard someone approaching on horseback. The last thing she remembered before slipping into unconsciousness was someone scooping her up and placing her gently into a wagon.

It was morning when Ellen finally opened her eyes to see five giggling little girls in white night dresses standing in a row before her. They looked like stair steps, the shortest perhaps two and the tallest one no more than six or seven. Ellen blinked again and again, not believing her eyes. Where was she and how did she get here? In the small cabin behind the angelic-looking girls stood a simple pine tree with a dozen homemade ornaments adorning it. Mentally, Ellen counted up the days since she had left home and suddenly realized that Christmas was just a few days away! She tried to sit and could not, gasping in pain at the unsuccessful effort.

Just then, Samuel, the man who had rescued her, came into the cabin. He told her that another train was due to come through the day after Christmas. If Ellen was well enough to travel by then, he would take her to the depot in town and she could resume her journey. But first things first—it was time for breakfast. There were wonderful smells emanating from the cast-iron stove in the corner of the cabin where Samuel's wife, Sarah, stood, making a small mountain of flapjacks. Ellen suddenly realized how hungry she was.

Ellen spent the next few days with this family while her body mended, and each day she felt a little stronger. She felt bad that she was burdening this young family with her problems, but there was no choice. She felt less guilty when she discovered she could actually be of some help by keeping the girls, whose names she could not keep straight, occupied while Samuel and Sarah went about their many chores.

Christmas Day dawned. Five small packages, one for each girl, had been placed beneath the tree during the night. Ellen had watched Sarah knit five little pairs of mittens by the firelight after the children were in bed, and she felt sure that this was what the packages held. Very useful and needed, but not the kind of present a child dreams of for Christmas.

After breakfast, the little girls scampered eagerly to the Christmas tree, gazing longingly at the gifts beneath it. Feeling very much like the outsider that she was, Ellen excused herself, saying that she needed to freshen up a bit. Sarah told her to use her bedroom, which was nothing more than a bed hidden behind a quilt hanging from the rafters. Ellen rummaged through her suitcase and found the package that she had carefully wrapped in flannel. She'd had little space for any "extras" in the case, but had made room for a few small treasures. She had brought some things from her childhood that she just couldn't bear to part with, two of her favorite dolls, a couple of picture books, and her reader from her first year of school. How odd that she brought five childhood items and there were five little girls here. Also in the package was the pocket watch that she had bought to give Jimmy for when he finally came home from the war, a pretty lace handkerchief that she had planned to carry on her wedding day and the beautiful brooch that Jimmy had given her the day he left. She tucked the brooch back into her suitcase and then carefully rewrapped the remaining seven items in the soft flannel.

She slipped back into the living area and tucked the package under the tree while no one was looking. She was slightly reluctant to part with her treasures, but she wanted desperately to show her appreciation to these people who were so willing to share what little they had with her, a perfect stranger. She was rewarded one hundred-fold for her spontaneous gesture by the looks of surprise and delight on their faces when they opened the unexpected gifts. But it was the gratitude in the eyes of the parents while watching the happy children that brought Ellen to tears.

Many years have passed since that unusual Christmas in 1864. Although Jimmy could never be truly replaced in her heart, Ellen eventually found love and happiness in her new home in the West. But even after all this time, thoughts of that Christmas Day so long ago would always bring a smile to her face. That was the only year that Ellen had not received a gift from a loved one. But it was the year when the gifts she had given had been the most appreciated and brought her the most joy. It truly is better to give than to receive!

PIN POINTS OF LIGHT

By Linda Dye

The piercing jangle of the phone caused a harried, flustered Sally to dry her dishpan hands and lower the burner beneath a simmering pot of beans. Her harsh "hello" projected a definite feeling of irritation.

There was a pause as Sally listened to the caller, tucking a damp tendril of hair behind her ear, before responding, "Frank, do you think you are the guardian angel for every Tom, Dick and Harry that comes along. Well, what can I say? If you insist. I will see you when you get here."

In approximately fifteen minutes, Frank arrived as Sally, still in her apron, was scurrying back and forth, covering and putting food in the refrigerator. Tomorrow was Christmas Day and fifteen family members from both sides of the family would have dinner at their house. There were casseroles to prepare, gifts still to be wrapped and bathrooms to be cleaned. Besides, UPS had not delivered her mother-in-law's gift, and now Frank expected her to go off on some wild goose chase to another town with a stranger who meant absolutely nothing to her.

As Sally hurried out the door, she took a deep breath, grabbed a plate of her homemade snicker doodle cookies and resolved to at least be civil. There waiting was her husband,

Frank, and a young, disheveled, baby-faced man, looking ill at ease as he extended his hand and introduced himself.

On the phone, Frank explained that the young man's car had broken down and was towed to a local repair shop. Parts had to be ordered and it would be several days before the car would be in operation again.

To stem the urge to scream, as she thought of all she had left undone, Sally made a feeble effort to engage the timid man in conversation as the miles clicked off. He revealed he was traveling from Virginia, where he had taken a job after college. His elderly, childless aunt and uncle had taken him in as a young teenager after both of his parents were killed in a plane crash. They were expecting him for Christmas, and he was so grateful to Frank for offering to make the hour and a half drive to see that he arrived at their house on time.

Sally felt some twinges of remorse as her mind processed the contrast of the wonderful, large gathering she and Frank would enjoy at their house tomorrow, with this man's sparse family gathering of only three. Thank goodness, due to Frank's insistence on helping a stranger, the older couple would not be alone on Christmas Day.

At their destination they were met by a polite, friendly elderly man and woman who insisted, "Come in and refresh with a cup of coffee before your return trip." As they gathered around the table, drinking steaming cups of coffee and eating Sally's Christmas cookies, she observed a special love flowing between the couple and the nephew. The conversation and interactions were warm and had a calming effect, that lulled away some of Sally's anxieties.

The asphalt stretched ahead of them. Twilight had brought on a crispness in the air. Pin point dots of star light began to appear in the inky black sky, and then, there in the distance was a brightly lit church steeple slicing through the darkness.

Cars surrounded the small church and families dressed in colorful, warm scarfs, hats and gloves, milled about an open field. It was evident a live nativity was about to take place. Without hesitation, Frank slowed and pulled to the side of the road. "Sally, I think we should stop long enough for this."

Why not. What difference can another hour make?

Sally and Frank stood side by side in the crowd, a ticker tape of chores waiting at home coursed through Sally's head. A quietness and stillness fell over the gathering and the sheep and cows began to make their way to the rustic lean-to, followed by a young Mary carrying baby Jesus with her husband Joseph by her side. The innocent babe wrapped in swaddling clothes was placed in the manger and lowly shepherds carrying staffs slowly approached the makeshift stable.

On a platform high above the scene, someone dressed in a rustic robe read the Christmas story from Luke in a strong, clear voice. "And it came to pass in those days, that there went out a decree from Caesar Augustus that all the world should be taxed."

It was then that Sally was overcome with emotion and there was a deep ache in her heart that welled up inside, as thoughts turned to the Christ Child who would later hang on the cross to pay for her sins, to the young man in need of a ride that she almost talked her husband out of helping, because she was too busy and to the elderly couple she almost ignored, because she was in a rush to return home.

Tears came to Sally's eyes and glistened on her lashes as she took her husband's hand and leaned in closer, resting her head on his shoulder. In her chaotic pursuit of perfection, she had almost let the important things of Christmas slip away. "Sally, what's wrong? Are you okay?"

"I am now. Thank you, dear man, for making me take the time to remember what Christmas is really about. I love you and Merry Christmas."

It's Christmas

By Maxine Cobb

It's Christmas, it's Christmas, what a wonderful time of the year, it's Christmas, it's Christmas, I wish it was here.

The Sears Roebuck Catalog had come in the mail. It was time to look in the wish book to see all the things there were to wish for. Everything that I could imagine, and lots more things I had never imagined, was in the pages of the big book called the "cat a log". I don't know where it got its name, but that is what they called it when they didn't call it "a wish book".

The best thing about it was the dolls and toys. We could daydream about these things, but they never came to our house in the mail.

The children at school were bragging about what they were going to get from Santa at Christmas.

We would look and daydream about what we would do with each of the new toys and dolls we heard the other children say they were getting. We knew we would not get the same toys and gifts they were getting, but our imagination ran wild with the thoughts of the joy those gifts would bring us.

Thanksgiving passed, and Christmas was a long time away. It seemed that each day Christmas got further and further away.

We were still looking at the "Wish Book" wanting things. Our list got shorter and shorter as we were told that we wouldn't get all the toys we wanted.

All this time my mother and older sister were sewing and crocheting, making us things for Christmas.

Doll clothes and clothes for us were being done while we were at school or outside doing chores or playing. We were never at a loss for things to pass our time. If so, Mama would quickly find something else for us to do.

As children, we never suspected where our new things came from because we saw no cloth around our house like the doll clothes or our new clothes.

Some things we got were "hand-me-downs" or from other places. My mother and my sister took the dresses and other clothes and added laces, buttons or changed the buttons, and added some crochet or pockets of another color to change the looks so the clothes were difficult to recognize by the other children or us.

One Christmas, I got a small item that looked like a pair of shorts and top sewed together with a loop on each side to hang it on the wall. It was a good place to store small clothes in. There was a pocket on the bib of the top that had a nickel in the pocket.

The thing we knew we would get for Christmas was a homemade fresh orange cake. The kind that was made from scratch, not the "out of the box" from the store that we have today. It was the kind you made from scratch where you measure out each ingredient one at a time and mix with a spoon, the old-fashioned way. Mama usually made the cake.

That year daddy made the Orange Cake. I do not remember why, but I remember helping him.

I remember helping roll and soften the oranges to get the fresh juices to put in and on the cake. The juice was put in a bowl with vanilla flavoring and sugar to sweeten the juice while the cake was cooking.

We had to eat red eye gravy for breakfast a few days to have eggs for cake.

He used the largest iron frying pan to cook the cake. There were three layers of cake about twelve inches across.

They looked like the large pones of cornbread that we had for suppers.

He put the juice of a whole dozen oranges in and on the cake, with the chunks of oranges on the top and between the layers. Then he crushed the peppermint candy and sprinkled it on part of the cake to make it pretty. He left a place on the cake without candy and put crushed pecans on that part, because some of the family did not like the candy on the cake.

This is the only time I remember my daddy cooking the Orange Cake.

We had an invalid sister, and Santa always came on Christmas Eve so she could be in on the opening of the presents. He left our Christmas gifts on the back porch, made a noise, and left. We all rushed to see about the noise and found all of our Christmas gifts laying there on the porch. We all liked our gifts.

A house full of people came the next day to see our Christmas and eat Christmas Orange Cake.

SUMMER MISCHIEF

By Linda Dye

As I settle in the easy chair, with my jump start for the day, a strong cup of steaming coffee, I focus on Great Grandmother's majestic vase in a nearby cabinet. Revered and treasured by our family, it has been passed from one generation to the next. The beautiful blue and white color is still vibrant. The first time people notice it, they are stunned by its regalness, just as my brother, Paul and I were as children.

Once again, I am a six-year-old playing house with my dolls, hidden behind the sofa in the forbidden living room of our rambling two-story house. It is late summer, but the cool morning air tinged with the fragrance of honeysuckles ruffles the curtains at the open windows, bringing a welcoming reprieve from the sweltering heat. Amid the shady copse, in the side yard, the jabbering of blue jays, in need of a referee, lends a note of frivolity and carefree abandon to my make believe play.

Suddenly, there is the unexpected patter of footsteps entering the living room. I crouch low, holding my breath, my hands clammy, fearing it may be mother, who will surely scold me if she discovers I am playing in a room, which is reserved for guest only.

I can hear my heart pounding over the noise of the jays, as I lay listening, hoping the footsteps will continue moving through the living room, but they come to a halt in front of the curio cabinet holding Great Grandmother's treasured vase. Paul and I have been forbidden to touch the vase over the years. Our pleas for just one touch were always met with a firm, resounding "No".

Even with my limited view, as I peek, hunkered down from behind the sofa, I can identify Paul's dirty, bare feet and stubbed toe. *Thank goodness it is not mother, but what is Paul doing in the living room?*

Suddenly, the latch of the curio cabinet clicks. The cavernous, quiet room magnifies the sound which echoes and reverberates, causing beads of nervous perspiration to form on my upper lip, in spite of the morning coolness. There is a hollow thud, then a crash with the tinkle of breaking glass. Paul lets out a desperate low moan, and I cower further down behind the sofa, fearing all the commotion will cause Mother to make an angry appearance. More sounds of broken glass, departing footsteps, and then quietness.

After a reasonable time, I slink from my hiding place, cautiously approaching the curio cabinet. There is now a gaping, empty space where Great Grandmother's glorious vase once demanded praise and admiration from all who passed through the living room.

Sensing a vibe of possible trouble in the air, I wasted no time scurrying to my room, closing the door, nervously contemplating the outcome of this disastrous situation. *Far be it from me to bring it to anybody's attention, after all I was disobeying mother by playing in the living room myself.*

Days went by without mention of Great Grandmother's vase. Sometime later, as I passed the curio cabinet, there it was, Great Grandmother's vase, back in its usual place. *How had Paul managed to pull this off right under mother's nose?*

There was never a word uttered between Paul and me concerning the incident. He was never aware that I was in the living room that summer morning. Our childhood was left behind, we went away to school, married and had children of our own, carrying certain memories from our youth with us.

Every Christmas, we returned to our elderly mother's home to celebrate the holiday and exchange gifts. Spirits were running high and peals of laughter and conversation flowed from one group to the next in the living room, where we were now allowed to gather. It was my turn to open my gift. The gold foil paper crinkled and crackled, as my eager fingers explored, red and green ribbons unfurled and layers of tissue paper were peeled away in anticipation. In shock and amazement, I was now gazing at Great Grandmother's prized blue and white vase.

My eyes locked with Paul's immediately, as we simultaneously gulped air as if sucker punched. After a noticeable hesitation, I was able to utter the appropriate words of appreciation. In admiring and looking at the vase, I noticed the faint, spider web pattern of cracks where the vase had been repaired by an eight-year-old locked away in the secrecy of his room many years ago. Mother's failing eyesight prevented her from detecting the damage to her beloved vase.

As I sit admiring the vase today, I think of the anxiety and agony felt by my eight-year-old brother, as his small, awkward tree-climbing, crawdad-catching fingers desperately rummaged in the junk drawer, searching for glue to make the necessary repairs and the ordeal he went through, working feverishly to bringing the jigsaw pieces of the vase back together again before Mother discovered its absence from the curio cabinet.

Now that Mother is gone, I know the perfect gift for Paul next Christmas. I look forward to our discussion of what took place that day so many years ago.

Christmas Wishes & Reality

By Ann Davis

My earliest memories of Christmas Eve are of my family opening our presents. We never did it on Christmas morning. I am not sure why we did it that way. Maybe it was because we lived on a farm and there was more work to do in the morning. Animals have to be cared for every day of the year. So that was the normal for us. As time went on and the family grew, there were grandchildren to consider as well. Their parents wanted to be home on Christmas morning.

We did not go to see Santa Claus, did not really talk much about him. I knew where the presents came from. My sister and I never got what we asked for when we were young. We wanted cap pistols, caps and a holster. We always asked for them, and we always got dolls. The only time we got to play with the guns was when we went to our cousin's house. He got a new set every year, so we played with the old ones. We played with the dolls a little during the first few weeks, and then we left them in the closet. Of course dolls really did little in those days. There were no Barbies with fancy clothes. They did not change colors or do anything much at all. Usually, if my sister's doll had hair at all, she cut it or tried to do something different with the hair. So it ended up looking sort of sad or like her head got caught in the gears of a machine that gapped up the hair. The doll never had a happy ending.

When we were finally considered too old for dolls, we got clothes. Of course, we needed clothes. But we wanted the latest popular John Romaine purse or a pair of Weejuns loafers. Nope, didn't happen.

But life goes on. We did not know it but it is good to learn early that life will not hand you everything you want. Most of the time you have to work for it and wait on it.

So I waited for my guns and holster until my senior year in high school. Every year we had a *senior's week* where we dressed as different people throughout the week. There was always a *little kid's day*. That day we dressed as a kid. So the morning of that day, I stopped by the Otasco store on the way to school. At last, there was my set of guns. Westerns were big on television. A show called "Have Gun Will Travel" was a big hit. The hero always had two guns, plus a small derringer he kept out of sight under the buckle. I wore them at school all day, with a cowboy hat, of course. It was a popular costume that day.

Most of the boys wore their old guns. I was the only girl and challenged to several duels that day. Usually a teacher did the countdown. As you can tell, things were different back then. During my last gun fight of the day, a boy sneaked up behind me and took both my guns. So I drew my small derringer and shot my opponent. Both the teachers watching from their doors collapsed, laughing.

Today that would not be possible. There would be all kinds of groups to protest and demonstrate. The girls who dressed like housewives would have today's feminists up in arms. There would be worries and concerns by people about sexist stereotypes. Fortunately for us, we were just having some fun that one special day before graduating and stepping out into an adult world. A good many of our male classmates would be in Vietnam by the next year. They would have to exist in a world that few of the rest of us could not imagine. Some would never be the same when they came home. Some went on to college, others to jobs, and some were married soon after graduation; many of them are still happily married. I am still in touch with lots of them. Like me, they remember with a smile that last week when we could be young and somewhat carefree.

I know this is not a christmassy Christmas story, but it does tell you what my Christmas wish list was when I was young.

Santa's Surprise Visit

By Carolyn Bond

With three small children in the house, the week before Christmas became quite hectic. Our oldest was a five and a half year old son, a daughter three and a half and another daughter almost two. This happened on one of those hectic nights.

My family had just eaten supper together and my husband took the three to give baths while I cleaned up and washed supper dishes. As he was first, the boy had finished his bath and was back in his room in his pj's, when I got to the bathroom. Just before the girls were ready to get out of the tub, the doorbell rang. I left the bathroom, went to the door and when I opened it–there was Santa Claus!

Who? Where from? I had no idea.

I invited him in, asked him to sit down and told him he would have to wait till we got the girls out of the tub and dressed before he could see them.

After all were in the pj's, we told them Santa had come and they needed to go sit on his lap and tell him what they wanted for Christmas. We had a house rule–each child could ask for anything they wanted, but they would only receive three wants. Our son sat on Santa's lap and mentioned four or five wants. The oldest daughter sat on his lap and mentioned eight or nine wants. But, the baby girl, when she saw that man in the red suit sitting in her daddy's chair, began crying and would only peep around the hall corner. She WOULD NOT go near him.

Santa stayed about half an hour. The older two were so tickled that Santa had come to see them, they even got out the Sears catalogue to show Santa exactly what they wanted. The only interest of the little one was for "him" to leave!!

We found out the next day that "Santa" was the husband of one of my mother-in-law's work friends. That Lady's husband always dressed as Santa for their church Christmas party, so he already had the outfit with a beard.

That night began as a big surprise—for me, as it was later for the kids.

GRANDMOTHER'S STAR

By Linda Dye

"HENRY! HENRY! It's time. Thanksgiving is over. Get on out to the storage building and bring in MY Christmas tree and the other decorations. I want to get ahead of the game and have plenty of time to enjoy MY tree. I won't be rushed by the hustle and bustle that will begin to gear up next week. I need time to decorate a beautiful tree."

"Martha, just hold your horses and let me put on my pants and shoes."

Henry shuffled out the backdoor, tugging on his pants as he went, making a statement of irritation by letting the screen door slam. Martha's scolding voice over the slamming of the screen echoed behind him, growing less piercing as he went. There would be no escape from Martha's demands until MARTHA'S TREE was decorated to perfection.

On his unhurried walk to the storage building Henry thought, *yes, the Christmas tree is Martha's tree. Only Martha can arrange the lights just right, only Martha can put each decoration in just the right place and only Martha can position her grandmother's treasured star, the crowning glory, at the tip-top of the tree.*

Methodically, Henry hauled box after box of Christmas decorations to the great room, where Martha waited with a sparkle in her eye and a ring of enthusiasm in her voice. Tree decorating was a task where Martha excelled and Martha's skills came to fruition. The time and effort that her passion required was not an issue.

Henry dutifully began to assemble the various sections of the tree, when all of a sudden Martha's hands flew in the air and a blood-curdling yell vibrated throughout the room. "Henry, there is a snake in the tree!" Henry jumped back, in a move he thought he could no longer execute, hurling the tree to the floor.

"Do something Henry. Don't just stand there while that monster slithers through our house."

By then Henry had composed himself as he replied, "Martha, there isn't anything going to be slithering anywhere. That is only the shed skin. That snake is long gone."

"You need to do something out there in that building to ensure this will not happen again. It makes me cringe to think that varmints are scurrying around disturbing my decorations."

By then Henry had removed the snake skin and had the tree assembled, so his response was a weak, resigned, "Yes, Martha."

The next step was crucial, the plugging in of the lights, and wouldn't you know it, there was a dark section where the lights were not burning. Martha was wringing her hands and moaning, "Oh no, oh no. Henry, you'll have to run up to Walmart and pick up a couple of strings of lights, while I unpack the ornaments."

Once again, Henry headed out the backdoor. His actions spoke volumes, stomping feet, furrowed brow and a ricocheting slam of the screen door.

At Walmart the aisles were crowded, Christmas lights were at the back of the store and there were no clear lights to be found. After consultation with a clerk, a section of clear lights was found and Henry made his purchase. Relief flooded over him as he reached the car, easing into the seat, ready to start the ignition, when the words white wiring written across the box caught his eye. *This will never do. The wiring has to be green.*

As Henry finally stopped in the driveway, with the two strings of white lights with green wires, he thought, *what else can go wrong?*

An impatient Martha was waiting, ready to go forward with the decorating. The large ornaments had been arranged on the sofa, with middle-sized ones on a table and last the small ones on the floor.

While Martha twirled and whirled, absorbed in her tree decorating activities, Henry took advantage of the lull in demands being directed at him and retired to the bedroom, kicking off his shoes and closing his eyes, drifting into a peaceful sleep.

He was jolted awake by shouts of, "HENRY, HENRY," coming from the front room. "Grandmother's star is missing. It is not here. Did you bring everything in from the storage building? This will never do. Get up! Go out and check the building for the star."

As Henry made slow, sluggish half asleep steps out the backdoor, his mind went to last year when the Christmas decorations were packed for storage. His desire to watch a ballgame on TV had caused him to delay taking the boxes to the storage building, leaving them in the open carport overnight. Could something have happened to Grandmother's irreplaceable star during that time? *Please spare me. Don't let it be my fault. Martha will never let me live it down.*

Martha immediately burst into sobs when Henry returned to the house and announced, "Martha, I did my dead level best to find that star, but it was nowhere to be found."

"I knew it. I knew it. Leaving my Christmas tree decorations on the carport overnight last year was a grave mistake. There is no telling what took place out there in the dead of night when no one was looking after my things. Henry Cooper, you have ruined my Christmas." Her scathing voice sent a chill up Henry's spine.

The next two days were not pleasant. Martha gave Henry the cold shoulder, and Christmas cheer was nonexistent. For a little relief Henry whistled for his old dog Gus, grabbed his shotgun and called to a sullen Martha, "Martha, Gus and I are headed to the woods for a little squirrel hunting."

"Take your time. Stay as long as you please. Dinner will probably be a sandwich anyway."

The day was pleasant and Henry drank in the silence and solitude. *A man, alone in the woods, with his dog and his shotgun is a wonderful thing. It does wonders for the soul. It clears the mind and puts things in perspective. Martha and I will work through the fiasco of the lost star.*

Henry looked up, hoping to spot a squirrel, but all he saw was a large crow's nest. As he was about to move on, something caught his eye. It was bright and sparkled. *No, it can't be. Could it possibly be grandmother's star? Crows are noted for being attracted to sparkly things. Could some cunning, innovative crow have stolen the star to decorate its nest from the decoration box as it sat on the carport. How can I find out?*

Henry raised his gun to his shoulder and fired two shots at the empty nest. His aim was good and the metallic object tumbled to the ground. Lo-and-behold, to his surprise and astonishment, it was the treasured star, still bright and beautiful, now perforated with a peppering of buckshot holes.

Poor Gus was puzzled and startled at their abrupt departure from the woods and he panted as he ran along, trying to keep up with Henry's hurried step and long stride as they headed for the house.

Henry crashed through the door shouting, "Martha, Martha, I found the star and you will never believe where it was."

As Henry told the story of the crow's nest, Martha sobbed, finally winding down to an occasional gaspy shutter and a snuffle. At last she spoke words Henry thought he would never hear, "Henry, I want you to put Grandmother's star on top of the tree."

"Martha, it's your tree and you have always been the one to place the star on the tree."

"Not anymore Henry. From now on it will be our tree."

Henry and Martha stood snuggled together, arms around each other, gazing at the completed tree. "Martha, I do believe this is the most beautiful tree we have ever had."

"Yes, Henry. I do believe the lights twinkling through the holes in the star set everything off. It's like they were always meant to be. I agree, it is the most beautiful tree ever."

LA NAVIDAD

By Elsa V Salazar Krauss

LA NAVIDAD? You may ask what is La Navidad? It is the feast day celebrating the birth of Jesus Christ.

A couple of days before Christmas my daughter asked: Mom, are we having pernil, buñuelos, y natilla? Of course, honey, you know those are essential for the menu on La Navidad.

Everyone has their own Christmas traditions, whether they are personal traditions, family traditions, or national traditions. In Colombia, Christmas is celebrated on December 24 at midnight and into the late hours of the morning on December 25th.

Let me share some of the ways that we Colombians celebrate Christmas.

I was born in Colombia, South America and even though I have been in the United States for 53 years, La Navidad is the most important tradition that I kept in my family. Colombia is a Catholic country and the tradition of la Navidad is considered a great feast celebrated with family and friends. Lights and decorations are put not only in the houses but all over the city and the country. Colombia is recognized worldwide for the Christmas lights, especially in the cities of Bogota, Medellin, and Cali.

DIA DE LAS VELITAS

Officially, La Navidad in Colombia starts with the celebration the day of “las velitas” (the little candles) on December 7, which is the eve of the celebration of the feast of “the Immaculate Conception”. The origin of this celebration was in 1854 when Pope Pius IX defined the dogma of the Immaculate Conception of the Virgin Mary. In anticipation for this event, people started lighting candles and it is celebrated differently depending on what region of the country you live.

The last town where I lived before traveling to the United Sates was Cali. The day of the velitas is celebrated in Cali by people coming out to the streets in their neighborhoods to put small candles and lanterns in the streets near their homes to “guide the way of the virgin”. With each candle that is lit, a wish is made to the Virgin for the coming year and thanks are given for the blessings she has bestowed during the year that is ending. This is a special celebration for me because my birthday is December 8 and I am very devoted to the Virgin Mary.

This unfortunately is not a tradition that I kept because simply it is not feasible to do here in the United States.

EL PESEBRE Y LA NOVENA DE AGUINALDO

These two traditions are also important and we still follow them at home. El pesebre is the “manger” or nativity scene mentioned in the Bible. Jesus was born in a manger where Mary, Joseph, angels, the three kings, and the shepherds are part of the story. This manger is set up before December 16 which is the day that the “novena de Aguinaldo” starts and continues for nine days until December 24. La Novena is a preparation or advent prayer for Christmas recounting the nine-month pregnancy of the Virgin Mary and Joseph. There are several prayers followed by singing “villancicos” or Christmas carols and enjoying traditional Christmas foods. When I lived in the city of Cali, Colombia, the novena was and still is celebrated every day in a different house around the neighborhood. This is a time to pray, and to meditate on the coming of Jesus Christ, but also to enjoy family and friends. There is food, dancing, and drinking as part of the celebration.

LA NAVIDAD

I grew up on a farm. Christmas was the best time of the year. We did not really have a traditional Christmas tree as is done in the United States but Dad, with the help of some farm workers, will put a big tree branch without leaves gathered in the country and set it in the open garage. This tree was filled with some decorations but mainly with presents for all the farm workers and their families. For us Colombians, el "Niño Dios" (the God child) is the one who brings the gifts. Children write him a letter and tell him what they want and Christmas at midnight, once the God child is born, they hope to find what they ask for under their pillow or at the foot of the bed.

One of my favorite Christmases on the farm was when I was about 6 years old. Dinner was served and everyone was enjoying the traditional meal. I couldn't eat well because I was more anxious to hear: "it is midnight! Baby Jesus is born". So I ran to my bed and to my surprise I did not find anything under my pillow. I was starting to cry when my mom said: "I think baby Jesus left something out in the front yard for you." So I ran out and sure enough, I had the most beautiful play house that my dad had built for me. It had a buffet for dishes and pots, a play stove, and a table with two chairs. I enjoyed this play house for years.

This tradition of the gifts under the pillow was followed by my children until they realized that mom and dad were the ones putting the presents there. So this tradition was changed for presents under the Christmas tree and later, as adults, envelopes with money on the Christmas tree.

As for decorations, we normally have the traditional Christmas tree and decorations in and out of the house. This year I went overboard decorating our house. It gave me a feeling of gratitude for the many things that God has blessed us with. Christmas lights on our roof and on the fence are the first decorations I put up right after we celebrate Thanksgiving. This year, the sense of love and unity was experienced within all our family members that were able to attend. Sadly, some have moved away, some live in another state, and some are overseas serving our country in the Navy.

Our Colombian Christmas tradition at our house has not changed drastically through the years. For some time now we, the adults, do not exchange gifts. In our families thankfully we have everything that we need and God has blessed us with so much that instead of presents we have "adopted" the game of the White Elephant which has been a delightful time after we have our traditional dinner which includes "pernil" or pork shoulder which I cook for several hours; "buñuelos" which are delicious cheese fritters made of corn starch, eggs and cheese and are the ones the most requested; "natilla", a sweet dessert made out of milk, corn starch, brown sugar, cinnamon and lots of love. The dinner is complemented with anything else people have brought to share.

All in all, this Navidad was special for the fact that we have not lost a member of the family due to Covid19 and everyone still has a job. For that we are very grateful.

I hope this short essay has given you a little information about the important Christmas holiday traditions in Colombia to celebrate Jesus' birthday!

Merry Christmas! Feliz Navidad!

The Best Gift is Love

By Pam Baker

Regina's heart swelled with happiness as she pulled back the red gingham kitchen curtain and watched the three next-door-neighbor boys return home after their unexpected visit with her. She loved those boys as if they were her own. She never had the joy of having a son. God had not blessed her otherwise happy marriage with children. She and Fred had always longed for a child, but as time passed, they came to terms with the fact that it was not to be.

Once Regina was so heartsick for a child that she went to the local orphanage and asked them if they had a child who needed special care. She was joyous when she brought home a six-month-old little boy who was having severe digestion/intestinal problems that had completely stumped the doctors. She prayed for help and guidance, and after a few short weeks under her care, she had the little boy totally cured. She took him back to the orphanage and the people there were amazed that the child was completely healthy. They asked Regina if she would like to adopt the little boy, and although she would have loved nothing more, she said no. She and Fred were very poor and she felt she could not give this child all that he deserved.

A number of years later, she again felt drawn to the orphanage. There she found another child whom the doctors had given up on. The little girl's head rested on her right shoulder; she was unable to hold it up. With this disability, no one would ever adopt her and she was doomed to a life without the love of a family. Regina's heart broke when she thought about the little girl spending her whole childhood in an orphanage, watching other children being adopted by loving families and her never being chosen. Even though her financial situation was still precarious, she had adopted the little girl and brought her home.

During the next few months, Regina worked with the little child she named Alice, massaging and manipulating her neck muscles. Miraculously, she was actually able to completely correct her physical defect. She and Fred lavished love on their Alice, but for some unknown reason, the child did not return their affection. Alice was a constant source of heartache and struck out on her own as soon as she turned 16.

Shortly after Alice's leaving, Regina lost her Fred. Except for a few caring nieces, she was now alone in the world. She filled her empty life with tending her vegetable garden and flower beds, reading any book she could get her hands on, and enjoying the tranquility of the nature around her country home. But she was very lonely.

That all changed one day as Regina was standing at the kitchen sink washing her breakfast dishes. She saw a car pull into the driveway at the empty house next door. She watched as a young couple got out of the car and began carrying boxes into the house. For some unexplained reason, she felt an immediate kinship with the young woman.

Regina was a very private person and didn't feel comfortable going next door to introduce herself. She spent the next few days watching out her kitchen window, hoping her neighbor would come outside. There was a large garden area between Regina's and the other house, and it wasn't long before Sue, the young woman, felt drawn to the garden.

Regina was very self-conscious about approaching her, but couldn't resist the urge to do so. When Sue saw Regina coming, something stirred in her as well. There was a huge difference in ages–47 years to be exact–but both felt an instant connection.

Over the years, the two grew to be the very best of friends. Three sons were born to Sue, and Regina loved those little boys as much as if they were her own. Sue would often bring the boys down to visit Regina and the boys had just as much fun as the two women, laughing at the silly stories they told and eating Pringles around the kitchen table. The boys loved going to see Regina. They never felt like they were visiting an old lady, they were visiting their friend.

Regina loved to look out her kitchen window and catch a glimpse of the boys playing. There were two other little boys who lived across the street who were also quite nice, but Regina was partial to Sue's boys. She felt the same about them as she felt about Sue–there was just something about them she couldn't help but love.

Each spring, Sue would plant flowers in Regina's flower beds when Regina grew too old to do it herself. Since Regina's birthday was in April, it was a perfect present every year. The flowers brought Regina great happiness, not only on her birthday, but every day all summer and into the fall as she watered them and enjoyed their beauty, knowing that they were a gift from her special friend.

But May always brought a little sadness to Regina each year. On Mother's Day, she would more often than not be forgotten by the daughter she had adopted. But there was one Mother's Day that made up for all the missed ones. Regina had woken that second Sunday in May feeling a little sorry for herself. But her sadness turned to instant happiness when she heard the familiar "yoo-hoo" outside her window, the greeting that always announced a visit from Sue and her boys. She hurried to the door as fast as her aged body would allow and was overjoyed to see the three boys with huge smiles on their faces and their hands mysteriously held behind their backs.

"Happy Mother's Day" they called in unison. Regina laughed through her tears as she ushered the boys inside. One by one, they produced the surprise behind each of their backs. The youngest went first. He had lots of stuffed animals at home and loved every one of them. It was hard to part with one, but he had chosen one of his beloved Pound Puppies to give to Regina. He was sure she would love it because he knew she had a little sock monkey she slept with every night. And she DID love it!

The boys had learned a lot about Regina from their visits with her. The middle boy knew well that Regina LOVED black jelly beans. No one in his family liked black jelly beans, so his Mom immediately picked them out and threw them away before putting the jelly beans in the candy dish around Easter time. This Easter, he had asked his Mom to please save them for him. She thought it was a strange request, but did as he asked. He placed all the black jelly beans in a zip-loc bag and tied a ribbon around it, saving it for a special gift for his friend next door. The look of surprise and delight on Regina's face when he handed her the jelly beans was all the thanks he needed.

The oldest boy grinned broadly as he brought out his gift from behind his back. It was clumsily wrapped in some pretty paper and tied with crinkly ribbon. Regina anxiously tore open the little package and found one Hostess Ding Dong inside. The oldest boy explained that he had saved this especially for her from his lunch box on Friday. Regina knew what a sacrifice it must have been for the little boy to do without this wonderful treat and save it for her, and his kindness and thoughtfulness filled her heart with happiness.

All four of them had such a great time that Mother's Day morning. Regina cut the Ding Dong into four pieces and they all sat around the kitchen table and enjoyed this fine "feast". They told stories and laughed and talked like the good friends they were. As they were leaving for home, each boy kissed Regina's soft wrinkled cheek and received a hug from her as she thanked them for giving her one of the most wonderful Mother's Days of her life.

After watching the boys run home to their lucky mother, Regina let the red gingham kitchen curtains fall back into place. She turned to survey the remnants of the party still left on the table and smiled. Some mothers get breakfast in bed on Mother's Day, or a trip to a fancy restaurant for brunch. Some receive a big box of chocolates or a bouquet of flowers. Still others might open a pretty package containing a luxurious bathrobe or pair of soft slippers. Very few would ever receive a used stuffed animal, candy that had once been destined for the trash can, or one Ding Dong. But very few would ever be any happier with their fancy gifts than Regina was with these simple ones given with love. Love - that's the best gift.

Christmas at Three

By Rhonda Trueman

On this winter's evening, I sort through boxes of black and white family photos to digitize. This project, put off until a vague someday, is finally underway. Using the development dates stamped on the back of these photographs, I sort them into loose chronological order. Minutes turn into hours as each photo I touch magically brings forth memories or transports my heart back in time.

In a photo dated January 1957, I see myself as three years old on Christmas Eve 1956. Adults are coming in the front door behind me, but only their legs and hands are visible. We have returned from our annual trip to McAdenville, NC, to see the Christmas lights. Our family gathers at my Grandmother's each Christmas Eve to celebrate. After dinner, we visit this tiny mill town with thousands of red, green, and white lights decorating immense fir trees. The sparkling trees line Main Street and circle a small lake. Floodlights surround a huge water fountain in the center of the lake. We park to watch the water dance and keep an eye out for Santa flying through the starry sky overhead. We never saw Santa, but I felt he knew we weren't at home because he would visit my grandparents' house early, leaving gifts to discover when we returned from McAdenville.

In this photograph, I am focusing on the gifts Santa placed under the tree. My face reflects surprise and glee as I pull off my scratchy woolen coat. My eyes sparkle, looking at the toys Santa placed under the tree and the gifts wrapped in colorful ribbons and snowy scenes. The tree is enormous and sparkles with silvery icicles thrown across its snow-flocked branches. The branches glow with colorful, warm lights, deepening the scent of evergreen throughout the house. Other aromas mingle in the air: cookies and cake; perfume and aftershave; coffee and cigarette smoke. My Christmas stocking is bursting with the sharp citrus smell of oranges and the sweet wintry smell of peppermints. I can hear the murmur of adult voices talking overhead, the sound of my Grandmother's laughter, and the soothing sound of my mother and aunts singing carols in three-part harmony.

In this one photograph, I revisit a three-year-old's perspective of Christmas and remember the joy of a loving family. It is Christmas 1956, and I am the happy center of the universe.

A Purr-fect Valentine's Day

By Pam Baker

February 12, 1999

Valentine's Day was only two days away, and Freddie still hadn't come up with an idea good enough to get Mary to finally notice him. She was the most beautiful girl he had ever seen in his whole life. He had loved Mary since the day she walked into his 2nd grade classroom that fateful sunny day last Fall. Even at the tender age of seven, he had known right away that there would never be a more perfect girl for him than the lovely Mary. She was absolutely perfect, from the band aid on her knee, to the geeky glasses, to the perky blonde ponytail highlighted in the warm September sun.

As fall turned to winter, Freddie found Mary possessed many additional desirable qualities other than beauty. She was one of the best readers in the class, rarely stumbling over a word when asked to read aloud. She never made a mistake in the weekly oral spelling bees. When they sang Christmas carols in music class, Freddie learned that Mary's voice was quite like how he thought an angel might sound.

And she was nice, too. When Brian dropped his bologna sandwich on the floor in the cafeteria, Mary immediately gave him half of her own peanut butter and jelly sandwich. When

Roger was making a Christmas card for his parents in art class and discovered he had lost his red crayon, Mary had quickly offered her own red crayon, telling Roger that she was done using it when Freddie knew for a fact that she was not. On the playground, Freddie observed that Mary would fearlessly swing higher than all the other girls. And when the bell rang and everyone ran to get in line, Mary could run even faster than most of the boys! Mary was just plain perfect - that was all there was to it.

Freddie sat at his desk in his bedroom and was supposed to be doing his phonics homework, but he couldn't get his mind off of Mary. Instead, he counted his meager pile of coins once again, hoping that by some miracle there would be more than the last time he counted. Nope—same as last count—only $1.43. How could he grab the attention of Mary with such a small amount to work with? Since the gift could not be large and impressive, it needed to be extremely meaningful. What could he do with that small amount that would show Mary how much he cared for her?

He wracked his brain for ideas. He remembered that whenever she brought a new folder to school, it usually had a picture of a kitty on it. Mary must like cats, so maybe he should start thinking of something along those lines. But with only $1.43 to work with, this was going to be almost impossible.

Then he had a brilliant flash of inspiration. Last summer, McDonalds had a Teenie Beanie Baby promotion when you bought a Happy Meal. Freddie had talked his Mom into taking him there a couple of times each week and by summer's end, he had collected all twelve of the cute little beanie babies. They were all tucked away in a shoe box in his closet, and Freddie seemed to remember that one of them was a cat.

He retrieved the shoebox from the closet and held his breath as he opened it and rummaged through the little treasures.

There it was—Zip the Cat!!! Oh, this is fantastic! This cute little black and white kitty would be a perfect Valentine gift for Mary. She was going to be so happy! And since it would cost him no money, he still had the $1.43 to spend. Again, the light bulb went off in Freddie's head - he would buy her a giant Kit-Kat bar! Oh, this was going to be perfect. Surely Mary would then like him as much as he liked her.

February 13, 1999

The next day, on his way home from school, Freddie stopped at the corner grocery to buy the Kit-Kat bar for Mary– 69¢. There was a display rack of Valentine cards near the door, and Freddie pored over them. Since Valentine's Day was tomorrow, they were pretty picked over and most of them were for grown-ups and were way too mushy. But hiding behind one of the really mushy ones was the one that he knew was made just for Mary. It was just a picture of a sweet little kitty and said, "You're Purr-fect!" and it was only 49¢. Freddie bought both and had money left over!

When he got home, he signed the card in his very best penmanship. He wrapped the card, the Kit-Kat bar, and Zip the Cat together in some red tissue paper, tying it all together with a pretty red ribbon. He was ready.

February 14, 1999

On Valentine's Day, Freddie could barely sit still in class. He watched the clock even closer than he normally did, willing the hands to move faster so that 2:00 could come and the Valentine party could begin. The clock must be broken, the hands didn't seem to move at all! This was harder than waiting for Christmas! Freddie became lost in thought, anticipating Mary's reaction to his gift.

He was happily startled out of his reverie when Miss Stock finally announced that it was time to put away their books and begin the Valentine festivities. As the whole class scurried to retrieve their exchange valentines from their desks, Freddie trembled with excitement–and then dread. Had he overdone it? Had he gotten too mushy? But it was too late now—he would have to plunge forward and hope for the best.

In art class last week, each member of the class had decorated a small box to sit on their desk to hold the valentines. All the children would deliver their individual valentines to the box on each student's desk.

As Freddie walked up and down the aisles, depositing his Valentines in the appropriate box, he almost backed out when he approached Mary's desk. But he had to give it to her. It was this or nothing, and "nothing" would be totally unacceptable. His hand shook a bit as he laid the gifts wrapped in the red tissue and tied in the red ribbon in Mary's box. He then hurried back to his desk and began to sweat and worry.

When everyone had returned to their seats, Miss Stock told the class they could now open their valentines. Freddie didn't touch his, his eyes were glued on Mary. Since she sat two rows over and three seats back from him, he could see her face and watch what she was opening. One by one, she opened little cards from her classmates. Some even had heart-shaped suckers inside, some held those little candy hearts.

Mary finally came to Freddie's. His heart almost stopped beating. Mary carefully untied the ribbon and opened the tissue paper. She smiled as she read the card. The smile turned to a big grin when she spied the giant Kit-Kat bar. But when she picked up Zip the Cat, the grin vanished. Her eyes widened with a look of surprise and another emotion that Freddie could not quite understand. And then she began to cry. Oh, no!!! This is awful! What had he done?

After what seemed like forever, she picked up the red ribbon and reached back to tie it around her ponytail. She then looked up and gave Freddie a brilliant smile. And even though there were tears in Mary's eyes, it was one of the happiest smiles Freddie had ever seen. She liked it!!! Maybe now she liked Freddie, too!!! He could breathe again–all was right with the world.

February 14, 2021

The years passed and Mary exchanged her skinned knees for long silken limbs and her geeky glasses for contacts that allowed you to clearly see her gorgeous blue eyes. The hairstyle changed, but the beautiful blonde hair remained. And today she was going to change something else–her last name. Today was going to be the happiest day of her life–the day she became Freddie's wife.

As she put the final touches on her hair and adjusted her wedding veil, she could hear the organ music softly begin, signaling that the ceremony was imminent. Her thoughts drifted back to that Valentine's Day 22 years ago, when she had been going through such a rough time in her young life. She had to transfer to a different school when she and her mother were forced to move from their beautiful home into a cramped apartment after her father died. She had tried to put on a brave and happy face at school, but inside she felt so empty and alone.

On top of grieving for her father and missing her friends at her old school, Mary had to say goodbye to her beloved kitten when they moved to the "no pets allowed" apartment. She had loved Mr. Whiskers, and he had become even more important to her in the days following her father's passing. The black and white kitten had been such a solace to her as he licked the tears from her face while she cried herself to sleep each night. Holding his warm soft body and listening to him purr had been very comforting to Mary, and she missed him oh so badly.

So, when she opened Freddie's gift that Valentine's Day so long ago, he had no idea what a healing and special present he was giving her. And now that sweet, sweet boy from long ago had become the man that she loved with all her heart and soul—the man who today would become her husband. And all thanks to Zip the Cat—purr-fect!!!

Manuhia

By Robert Vasvary,

"I consider myself in the top two percent of the luckiest people in the world," a friend once told me while we were sipping whiskey on my boat. I feel the same way after visiting Easter Island, one of the most remote inhabited inlands in the world; Rapa Nui, as the islanders call it, Isla de Pascua in Spanish.

In 2006, I was working in Santiago, Chile and was feeling alone, not being very fluent in Spanish. This was only weeks before meeting my future wife, Nicolina, with whom I am still happily married fourteen years later, and we have an eleven-year-old son, Ethan. We are soulmates and this Holiday tale played a role in that.

One Thursday evening in the hotel, I was bored and went to the bar. I ordered a drink and noticed a couple there beside me speaking English. I immediately spoke up. The guy introduced himself as Mark from New Zealand and his wife Ra'a, a true descendant of the island. Her father was the Mayor! They were a charming couple, and we discussed what we were doing here. They were returning to the island where they were to resume work on their new home after a much needed getaway. After a few drinks, he leaned over and whispered to his wife, then turned to me.

"We are flying out tomorrow. We would like to invite you to come over this weekend," Mark offered.

I accepted their offer and when I returned to my room that night, I immediately booked a flight leaving the next day after work. This was a once-in-a-lifetime opportunity!

When I arrived at the airport on Easter Island, I was surprised by the dirt floors in the terminal and a donkey there with a Lei around its neck. Scanning the terminal, I did not see them. I was getting nervous when I heard Mark call, "Rob, over here!" Mark and Ra'a were standing beside the donkey. I raced right over. Ra'a slid the lei off the donkey's neck and put it on me.

We grabbed my bags and headed for their Jeep. The island was magnificent! Moments later, we pulled up to a quaint Tiki bar with Reggae music playing. Their friend Steve, a local, had returned home from Manhattan, finally sickened by modern society, and had just opened up his own restaurant. We had a few beers and some hamburger Ceviche (yes; I know it sounds gross but after an hour soaked in lemon; it is fabulous) and settled in. I immediately felt like a Pirate on a remote island mingling with the locals and a few worldly travelers.

From there we stopped by to visit Ra'a's family and when we pulled up, two men came out, their arms dripping in blood.

"Not to worry," talking to me while looking at them, "We just sacrificed a goat for my niece's birthday." We didn't even leave the car; which was a bit of a relief for me. They said goodbye, and we headed for their home, which they described as their very own Outback, on a plateau with miles of soft rolling grassy plains.

Suddenly, we were greeted by two eager dogs, one acting ferociously, and my defenses went up again.

"Rob, this is our family. Meet Jesus and Mary," Mark spoke with pride.

Mary was the wild one, and when she calmed, we exited the Jeep. Their home was made of concrete blocks and had no windows yet. That was their next project, they informed me apologetically. We walked into the house to dirt floors. Mark apologized for the crudeness and showed me around while telling me his plans to finish their dream home.

Despite the primitive feel of this little island, it was the most tranquil setting I had ever seen. As the sun was setting, Ra'a was preparing a dinner of local cuisine and a selection of meats to grill. Mark and I started the campfire while the dogs played. Right at dusk, the sun looked bigger than I had ever seen, the size of the World Fair globe! Everything out here on this small island all alone in the Pacific Ocean everything was larger than life!

After a grand dinner, we sat around the fire talking about worldly things and drinking while Mark strummed on his guitar. We started making up songs; the peaceful setting lending to limitless creativity and expression. At one point, I looked up and remarked how bright the night sky was, especially the cloud directly overhead. Mark just laughed and said,

"Bob, that is no cloud mate, that is the Galaxy!"

I had never ever seen so many stars in my life, and I had a front-row seat to the best view of the Milky way few have ever had! I leaned back, fixated on the view long enough to remove my soul from the world's civil chains and worries. As he played his guitar, I began to sing, and we made a song.

"What should we name it?" I inquired. "It has to be a Rapa Nui-an Word."

"Let's call it Manuhia," said Ra'a. "It means welcome."

After many cold beers and incredible conversation, we finally retired for the night. I still have the recordings of the song.

The next morning, we set off in the Jeep for a tour of the island. The first stop was a crater on the Northeast end. It was colossal! From there we headed around the island counterclockwise across grassy stretches of land with wild horses running along the beach until we came to a park and headed inland to a hillside where I saw my first moai, a rock sculpture that was at least 30 feet tall. Standing beside it, I felt infinitesimal. Mark narrated as we walked, explaining that each generation would try to outdo the last by making them larger. He said they would use trees and roll them to their location, which is why the island was deforested through the years. He went on to say that the original tribe's intent was to warn visitors. That is why the moai were facing outward to declare that anyone visiting here was not to interact with the women of the island. On the hillside, there were some that were still in the ground.

"The last few tribes must have become overzealous and made them so big they could not get them out of the ground," Mark commented.

As we continued around the island, we came upon the most amazing cluster of statues. "These are the ones most have seen in historical magazines," Mark added.

They also had hats carved on them. He explained that when a typhoon came and knocked them down, the Japanese came and resurrected them, preserving the monument.

Our last stop before returning to town was a beach where the moai were facing inward, the only ones on the island in this position. Ra'a explained that these were to remind the women not to interact with visitors.

The culture of this remote island waypoint has been preserved for many centuries because of these rock statues and the Rapa Nui have maintained their bloodline very well.

Rendezvous of Farewell

By Bonnie McAlarney

The nurse at the door greets me with a smile of understanding. "You've come a long way... from Georgia. Right?"

I nod. In response to my question with regard to the Covid mask I am wearing, she pulls a chair over to the bedside and says, "I'll give you some privacy for a while." She leaves the room.

I sit beside the hospital bed hoping to connect with the wasted body at rest amid hospital sheets... searching the face, colorless and time-washed by a long life and now loneliness due to isolation from family and friends. Within her aches a longing to be at home with family that circumstances will not allow. The blue eyes express a slight response of recognition and the nose like our dad's, juts from the withered, ashen, zombie face. We are, each of us, morphing into our mother as in her final years and days.

The hand I hold, tattooed with purple bruises from IV needles, is soft and warm, as though her life source resides there. I place kisses as gifts of my life-time sister-love on the forehead and cheeks of the face encircled with white cotton candy hair. She may not remember the one kiss enfolded in her right hand for keeps, but I will. Speaking those "best of my words" collected and rehearsed in my mind or on occasion having been spoken or written, seem to fall on the blank screen of her face; her eyes never leaving mine.

"How long can you stay?" she whispers.

Her lips reveal the escape of her real self out of the darkness of Alzheimer's captivity, if only for this five minute visit as sacred as the Magi from the east.

It is the Monday following CHRISTMAS DAY, Friday, December 25, 2020.

The last time I had seen my sister Mimi was three and a half years earlier when her twin great-granddaughters were born on MEMORIAL DAY 2017. She was ninety-six and doing well, but with hints of dementia. At that time, my husband, older daughter and I had traveled to Pennsylvania to meet the new babies and visit with family members still living there. We had moved South fifty-two years earlier in response to an employment opportunity.

When Mimi reached ninety-nine, our youngest son made a promise. "Mom, next year, if Mimi reaches one hundred, I will take you home for her birthday!"

The next year came, 2020... the worse year of my life and the worse year of Mimi's life as well as many, many others. A year of troubles and sorrows for everyone. There had been subtle beginnings over the years, becoming more evident as time moved on. Unrest smoldered with riots and violent destruction. Then the plague of Hatred roared into being magnifying the disorder.

Mimi entered Gracedale nursing home weeks before 2020 began, missing THANKSGIVING and CHRISTMAS celebrations at home with her family.

Topping off the strife, the world-wide COVID-19 virus took over, full-blown within months like a swarm of locust blanketing the earth, devouring and destroying people's lives.

Visitations of residents in nursing homes were halted by lock-downs and a hibernation was forced on us all.

In April Mimi contracted the virus battling and surviving the challenge with not one warm visit by family or friends. Only her faithful Aide was there, a wonder-worker who stands in the gap during sickness and health, reality and delusion, life and death; the go-between for the families and those lost in the seeming desert of abandonment.

These gifted people reach into their closet of servant-hood, put on the necessary garment like a priest at the altar, becoming hope and assurance to those deserted and those restrained by circumstance.

Stephanie's hands became the warmth, affection, healing, and encouragement. Her smile of support initiates the bond erased from reality. Her voice brings to life the letters, cards and gifts. She arranges phone calls and virtual visits by employing the magic of the tech world to present the family with glimpses of their loved one. Hers is the life that sustains her patient and comforts the family.

Stephanie became the heart and hands that nurtured Mimi, stirring the lifelong senses of maternal bonding and family life from decades past, through EASTER, MOTHER'S DAY, MEMORIAL DAY, INDEPENDENCE DAY and other less important holidays.

We were excited when at the beginning of October the lock-down had been relaxed and our plans for Mimi's 100th birthday, October 24, budded in our hearts and minds. The youngest son, older daughter and I began packing our bags in preparation for the long awaited occasion and the trip across several states.

The beginning of that week... the week of her birthday, our high flying balloon of anticipation was deflated by word that increases of covid cases meant the closing again of the home. The traveling bag sat beside my bed.

On Mimi's special day... her 100th BIRTHDAY... a century of living, Stephanie took out her magic paint box of colors, brushes and combs attempting to discover and recreate the beauty at the heart of her charge, stirring the youth, reviving the life that had been.

Wearing her silken floral blouse, her hair bouffant, her face radiant, Mimi sat in her chair inside the window of the building with eight members of her family outside looking in at the beautiful lady come to life by the hand of the artist. There were gasps of awe and wonder, "She's beautiful!" wherever the photos of Mimi appeared over the tech waves such as Facebook.

Mimi reached her hands toward the window, reflecting the little ones and their brothers, and all the babes she had swaddled, cuddled and fed the morsels of life over many, many years. Only her eyes could capture the joy in real time, memories salved the longing to touch and hold each one again.

Mimi's cake with candles was shared behind closed doors in the confines of her substitute home, with no family members present.

***

Man's questionable intentions have upended even the rules of living and dying. This world seems twisted and broken.

One more time the ban is lifted on visitation for Mimi. A time when we might see her face to face. Being moved to hospice care because of her condition, the travel bags and passengers are loaded in the car at noon on Sunday, 740 miles from Mimi. Time goes quickly over the ribbons of highway as we reminisce, traveling through memory's years… while Mimi, too, speaks to those around her of being in Georgia. Four souls finding each other in the folds of time, love's magnetic pull refreshing the wonders of the past.

By Monday afternoon, through five states between Georgia and Pennsylvania, I am at her bedside for that five-minute rendezvous of farewell. We leave on Tuesday morning on our return over the same highway from a journey more like a dream than reality… back home in our beds that night; Mimi in Gracedale Nursing Home… like a blink of an eye.

***

Mimi and I stand on the threshold of eternity trusting that the rules of heaven since the beginning of time, still apply to eternity. We believe that unadulterated Love and Truth... The God who is Love and Truth Himself will welcome us home to one long, forever, holiday.

“

Sometimes it's a little better to travel than to arrive.

”

–Robert M Pirsig, Author
Zen and the Art of Motorcycle Maintenance

Motorcycle Road Trip Adventures

By Amanda Cantrell

My boyfriend, Odie, and I rode motorcycles. That's how we met; I wanted to ride his motorcycle. Well, we met at church, but we started talking because I wanted to ride his motorcycle. Then, we went out on a date, and that's how we ended up going together. He had two motorcycles. A Kawasaki he rode for speed, and a BMW. Because I was a single mom, it took planning for us to have time to ride.

My cousins also rode motorcycles. On New Year's Eve 1999, my mom agreed to babysit my daughters, so we got together with my cousin and her husband and rode into the new year, new decade and new century.

One weekend, we headed to the Blue Ridge Mountains. It's a popular place to ride motorcycles because of the curves and the views. Some roads are favorites among bikers. Like the one we took, called The Diamondback (North Carolina Highway 226A.m) that crosses the Blue Ridge Parkway and has 190 turns in 12 miles.

Two weekends later, we rode through the Chattahoochee and Nantahala National Forest, and through the Cumberland Gap into Kentucky. We would stop and look out over the beautiful vistas, and climb the trails. We climbed a trail that was spiraled such that every few feet we rounded a curve and crossed the state line. We took turns getting our picture taken laying across two states.

We left the Nantahala and went through the Cumberland Gap, where Daniel Boone cleared and used to go West. Only we passed through a tunnel–the first time I saw Kentucky it looked like a tunnel. But oh, how beautiful it was once we emerged! The grass is green as green can be, just rolling hills and mountains full of trees. The sky was as blue as a sky gets with big puffy clouds.

There was one place where there was a white farmhouse, a red barn, and, of course, a white picket fence. It was so beautiful I wanted to take a picture, but this was before camera phones were in everyone's hands. My prosumer camera was in the saddle bag being safe, and I missed one of the best pictures I never took. I still have that beautiful picture in my memory.

There was another place in Kentucky I wished I had easy access to my camera. There, for the first time, I saw Belted Cows. Their nick name is Oreo Cookie Cows because from the shoulders forward they are black and from the flanks backward they are black, but like an Oreo Cookie, they are white in the center. I loved these cows from the moment I first saw them. When I got home, I looked them up. They originate from Scotland–so do I. That makes them even more special to me.

That night was interesting. I was freezing! He was hot… I had on jeans, shirt and sweatshirt and two pairs of socks. I was under all the thin covers, then we spent the night and my goodness, he was hot and wanted the air conditioning on. I was freezing to death, so I was under all the covers of my bed. Odie took the two covers from his bed and put them over me. I was still freezing, and he was in a t-shirt and shorts and sleeping next to the air conditioner.

Sunday morning, we went to Corbin, Kentucky and to the first Kentucky Fried Chicken! It wasn't open on Sundays, but we looked in the windows and took pictures then headed home.

The Blue Ridge Mountains are truly blue. Trees put the blue in Blue Ridge Mountains. They release isoprene into the air that makes a blue haze on the mountains. The mountains look to me like God plucked the earth up like I would a tablecloth, making wrinkles in it. The rivers are so cold and clear and you could drink water just straight out of the ground. The colors in the fall are more beautiful than words can say.

On the way home, we had traveled this particular section of highway before and knew there were four or five different roads on one strip of asphalt. The divisions were marked the first time… but, that Sunday afternoon, camera still safe in the saddlebag, there were no clear divisions. There was not a cement plastic or saw horse divider. Not a line, not a stick or a twig! Just ten lanes of several roads going back-and-forth side by side, for a mile, maybe more. It was scary. We just went straight and prayed everyone else knew where their road should be. I will never understand how they could pave that many roads together on one bit of pavement with no sign where individual roads were.

I was so tired I hooked my left arm over Odie's shoulder and put my right hand under his arm around his waist and I grabbed my wrists with each hand. Odie held his arm over mine. When I was sure I had a good firm grip, I put my head on the back of his shoulder and slept for miles on the way home. Later, when I told him I did this; he was shocked! He explained that when he told me to do that; he was kidding! He said, "You could have fallen off!"

I told him, "No, if I hadn't slept, I could have fallen off. I was locked in pretty well."

Now I'm warm at home and all is well.

INDEPENDENCE DAY

By Sharon Wynns

"I am independent." Julie waved the small flag she had constructed of yellow gauze, then placed it beside the stone cairn in the middle of her garden. It was built from smooth river rocks she had gathered years ago. By balancing the different sizes and shapes on top of one another, it created a tower effect. The base was a large piece of flat black granite, polished on one side, that she had discovered in her creek.

A nearby quarry operation turned the raw granite into headstones. Through the years, trimmings and rejects were piled up and used by the county for road maintenance. Below her house, by way of two sizeable pipes, the creek passed beneath the road. The county dumped the granite trimmings around the pipes to shore up the roadside. Prior to these two pipes, only one had been there. Flood waters often washed the granite away–and finally, the road. There was an endless supply of these washed away pieces all down the creek.

Beside her, Kate held her green gauze flag to her breast, saying "May my heart remain open." Bending, she placed it beside the smaller stone cairn she had just assembled, then turned to Julie. "Just what do you have in your mind… now that you have claimed your independence?" She grinned at her longtime friend. “It seems to me you’ve always lived a *strongly* independent life.”

Julie led the way back to the lounge chairs set facing the horizon. Between them was a small table holding a bottle of Merlot and two wineglasses. It was The Fourth of July. Kate joined Julie in watching the fireworks set off in the city park every year. It lay just over the low ridge opposite to where they were now seated. Julie laid back her head and closed her eyes.

Minutes passed, and Kate finally gave Julie’s leg a friendly nudge with her foot. “C’mon old lady, don’t fall asleep on me.”

Julie chuckled, opened her eyes, and turned to her. “Not sleeping, just thinking, remembering.”

“Remembering what?”

“All those long years ago when I first moved here. I set up that cairn. It symbolizes the life path I chose; the one that brought me here.”

Kate shifted to her side. “And that’s how we first came to know each other. My boys and I were hiking along our dirt road in the mountains; and there you were, this tiny woman, carting rocks up the steep riverbank. When we stopped to say hello, you explained you were using them to line flower beds and to build a cairn. So, we helped you gather more.”

“And your boys… they were what, eight and ten? They wanted to build a cairn, too.”

“You drove us to our house, shared some rocks and our lunch. The rest is history.”

Julie poured the wine, handed Kate one fine-blown flute, and raised the other in a toast. “To that wonderful history.” Their glasses clinked and a high clear chime resonated as they sipped and settled back. The first bright lights lit up the sky and a synchronic “Oh!” escaped them, bringing a smile to each face.

Distant booms and crackles accompanied the brilliant offerings before them. They watched in companionable silence until Kate broke it by asking, "So, why this renewed claim of independence?"

Tiny solar star lights were strung through the branches above them and lit Julie's silver-streaked hair. She took one long strand and began to weave a narrow braid. Kate recognized this habit of contemplation and waited for her response.

"I don't know if you remember my original purpose in building my cairn."

"No, not really."

"It symbolizes the path I chose that brought me here… that it was the right path."

"Thanks for refreshing my memory… but what does it have to do with your claim of independence now?"

"Well. I think I'll start with this. I recently read a poem by Parker Palmer; he talks about how everything in life eventually falls away. Friends, work, things we've accomplished… or didn't, feeling good, feeling bad."

Kate nodded her white-haired head in agreement. "The older I get, the truer that is."

"So, everything but this one thread falls away. This one thread that, without realizing it, we've followed all our lives." Julie blew out a steadying breath. "I'll try to share what he said, but my words won't be as elegant as his. He said that this one thread runs through everything we've ever done or been. It strings it all together."

Kate knew Julie's thoughts went beyond the everyday events of life. Beyond—and deep. She enjoyed their conversations. Often, she came away with significant thoughts or ideas that she could apply to her own life. Kate sat in quiet anticipation, looking forward to what Julie had on her mind–and heart–on this light-filled, celebratory night. Before them, a brilliant white lights exploded high up, then fall earthward in a sparkle of myriad colors.

Julie took a sip of wine, then set it aside. “Palmer says the thread runs through our lives and stays all the way to the end… but doesn’t really end. We’re all following our own thread, doing our own thing, but they don’t end. Because it’s part of the whole… part of everything. Oh, how did he put it?” Julie glanced away, then looked at Kate, her eyes reflecting the tiny stars above them. “Here it is. He called it the ‘boundless whole.’ Boundless, but it’s where all our threads merge.” She spread her arms wide, shaking them for emphasis. “It’s… it’s this magnificent tapestry where we’re all woven together.” Dropping her arms, she continued. “He called it a masterpiece.” Her voice softened yet emphasized that last word.

Kate felt tears spring to her eyes. “That’s… that’s beautiful.”

Julie reached out and took Kate’s hand in hers. “I know.” Twinkly stars now reflected in both their eyes. Releasing their hands, they turned back to the display before them. Each sat in peaceful silence until Kate asked, “So, how does this relate to independence?”

“That’s my thread. That’s the one I’ve been following. It’s the one I am weaving into the tapestry. It’s my contribution to the whole.”

“It’s your ‘trust yourself’ thread.”

“It’s so much more than trusting myself. It’s about trusting everything. It’s practicing not being afraid of my life… of allowing myself to be easy with my life.”

“Ha! Easier said than done. Try being easy with a marriage of 42 years being tossed aside by an ungrateful… I want to say the ‘b’ word, but I won’t.” Kate released an angry sigh, then shook her head. “Sorry…” Now her voice held tears.

Julie’s touch was gentle yet firm as she placed a steadying hand on Kate’s arm. “Darling friend, please look at me.”

Kate’s view of Julie was blurred. She blinked hard several times, determined not to lose sight of this woman who cared for her, who had become the sister she never had. With her free hand, she wiped her tears away and allowed herself a small smile. “Okay, oh wise one, lay it on me.”

Julie chuckled. Kate always sought to bring humor to whatever her life held. She loved that about her. But there was something she admired above all else. Something she had watched Kate apply time and again when faced with challenges. Julie hoped she could find the words to soothe and encourage her now. Kate was hurting. The truth was all Julie had to offer her.

Swinging her legs around, she kneeled beside her friend and enveloped Kate’s hands within her own. “Everything falls away.” Kate’s hands stiffened, but she didn’t withdraw them. “Everything falls away but this one thread. It runs through all that we experience, think, feel.” She looked deeply into Kate’s eyes. “I want you to hear this, Kate. We all follow our own thread. Palmer didn’t say anything about it breaking. It remains to the end. Yours remains, even now.”

“But what is it?” Kate shook her head in frustrated confusion.

“You know. You said it earlier when you placed your prayer flag beside your cairn.”

Kate continued to shake her head, finding it hard to accept what Julie was saying.

“I’m not going to say it for you, Kate. You need to claim it for yourself.”

Giant bursts of light drew their attention to the horizon. Blazing, dazzling, shining with manifold hues, one, two, three at a time. The grand finale. "How appropriate!" Julie laughed. "Go ahead, Kate, claim it!"

Kate rose from her chair and reached a hand to Julie, who stepped alongside her. "Yes!" said Kate. "Let's both make our claim." Hands still clasped, they raised their arms to the heavens. Silhouetted against a twinkling rainbow that fell to earth in wild abandon, they shouted: "My heart is open! I trust my life!"

A Loving Mother and Son

By Linda Dye

The mourners quietly filed down the hill, each caught up in their thoughts of Julie McCoy's death. The news had spread, early morning July Fourth, like a dust devil racing and twisting across a newly plowed southern field. How can a mother and son, both, be taken away in the short span of two years, both on the Fourth of July?

Julie's life had been hard. A controlling, demanding, abusive husband had finally walked out on her and their five-year-old son four years before. Julie was devastated and financially destroyed, grasping for solutions and resources to keep the two of them in a home and provide food and clothing. Fear of failure was a constant. One bobble and she would be like the car that all four tires blew at once.

The struggles were never ending, but Julie worked hard, was frugal, and kept a positive attitude for the sake of her son, Jason. Finally now, four years later, Julie was offered a lucrative job in a nearby small town. There was a glimmer of hope for vacations, eating out and splurging on fun things. Julie was excited as she made preparations for the move. "Jason, be sure to check your closet, make sure everything has been packed. Bring those boxes downstairs."

As a nine-year-old boy, Jason dreaded the move. Changing school and leaving friends behind caused him to have misgivings, but he loved his mother and knew she was doing what was best for them. She would always be there for him. "Mom, do you think I will make the baseball team in Townville?"

"Sure, Honey, you are a great player." Julie put her hands on her hips and contorted her face into a stern, angry look. "They will hear from me if you don't make the team."

Jason laughed at his mother. She had a way of dispelling his doubts and worries. He was lucky to have such a great mom. She tried extra hard to make up for him not having a father.

Jason was the reason Julie could endure so many difficulties and keep up her spirits. At least one good thing came from her troubled marriage. She was blessed with a handsome, smart son who loved his mother.

Townville was a godsend for Julie and Jason. They joined the Presbyterian Church, singing the old, familiar hymns each Sunday morning and taking part in the various activities that were offered. People accepted the new family and included them in their get-togethers.

The McCoys became a part of the small, close community, attending parties and celebrations throughout the year, and in time, Jason became the star baseball player for the Townville Tigers, just as his mother had predicted.

The years slipped by with Julie and Jason relishing their idyllic lifestyle, surrounded by a bevy of friends and neighbors, who included and watched over the McCoy Family. Julie marveled at the way her life had turned around and been enriched. She was grateful for her blessings.

It was at a wedding reception, that Julie's best friend, Marty, introduced her to a handsome man by the name of Richard

Toole. Despite her resolve to never be involved with another man, she felt a strong attraction to Mr. Toole and was pleasantly surprised when he called the next day, inviting her to dinner and a movie.

Soon, Richard was a frequent visitor at the McCoy household, attending Jason's ball games and helping Julie with home repairs and car problems. Julie was puzzled by the feelings she began having for Richard and questioned what the future might hold.

On a warm, full moon night in June, eight months after their first date, Richard took Julie's hand as they strolled around the moon lit neighborhood. "Julie, I have been thinking."

"Richard, my goodness, you sound so serious."

"Well, the truth is, I am serious. I have come to the conclusion that my life cannot be complete without you and Jason being a permanent part of it. You know how close Jason and I have become, and you also know how much I love both of you. I want the three of us to make a life together."

"Richard, what are you trying to say?"

"Julie, Julie, sweet Julie. I am asking you to marry me."

Julie stopped in her tracks. No words would come. Tears began to flow. After a long pause she said, "I never thought I would want to marry again, but you have made such a difference in my life and Jason's life. I love you too, Richard, and want to marry you more than I can ever tell you."

Jason, friends and neighbors were overjoyed with the news of Julie's and Richard's engagement. A Fall wedding was in the makings. Julie's best friend, Marty, enthusiastically agreed to be matron of honor.

In Townville, it was a tradition for everyone to gather at Pebble Lake to celebrate Independence Day. Sumptuous picnics were prepared to be spread out on large wooden tables and shared by everyone, the high school band played traditional Sousa marches and children and teens played and swam in the roped off swimming section of the lake, while adults milled about visiting with old and new friends.

As night came on, everyone sat, appetites satisfied by delicious food, warmed by the sun in anticipation of the spectacular fireworks that were to come. Only the children still scampered and ran about, carrying helium filled red, white and blue balloons, squealing and laughing, followed by harried parents trying to reign them in.

Julie knocked on Jason's open door. "Jason, it's time to rise and shine. Richard will be here shortly to take us to the lake. What a glorious day for a Fourth of July celebration. While you are at it, see what you can do about cleaning this room. You would think a herd of pigs had been rooting in here."

Jason rolled over, yawned, and stretched his lanky fourteen-year-old frame. "Mom, we are always early for everything. All I will need is my swimsuit and a towel. I'll be ready in a sec. Did you make those chocolate cookies I like?"

Julie never missed a chance to please her adorable son. In fact, some said she spoiled him, but he was not demanding or rebellious, as many spoiled adolescents seemed to be. "You know I would never forget to make your chocolate cookies. They are already packed in the picnic basket. Now up with you, and do something with this room."

The park was alive with activity when they arrived. Julie smoothed down the new knee shorts and pretty shirt she had purchased last week on a shopping trip with Marty. She had resisted the purchase, but when Marty said, "Julie, those shorts make your legs look a mile long," the deal was sealed. She had noticed the approving looks Richard had been giving her since they left home. Julie felt good about her appearance and was glad she had splurged on the new outfit.

Julie and Richard made their way to a large shade tree where a waving Marty and her husband, Carl, stood. Jason had parted company with the adults as soon as he spied his friends at the lake shore, giving his mom a jaunty wave as he trotted toward a group of young people.

The afternoon wiled away, everyone relaxed and celebratory. Julie initially ignored an excessive amount of movement at the lake, but then someone speaking Jason's name caught her attention. Immediately there were shouts of, "We can't find Jason."

Julie bolted from the lawn chair, arms and legs flailing as she raced toward the lake. A swooshing sound was made as Julie's shoes were sucked from her feet by the muck at the bottom of the lake as she reached the water. Julie was oblivious and paid no heed to the fact that her attractive new shorts and shirt became embarrassingly transparent when wet. An animal like sound, a cross between a moan and a scream, came from Julie and resonated above other sounds, as she struggled forward.

Richard was finally able to wrap his arms around Julie and pull her back to shore, where she thrashed and screamed, "Jason, Jason. My sweet boy," collapsing in the sand. Her mind was like an electrical arc that sparked and jumped in rapid succession from one thought to the next, remembering this morning. W*hy did I wake him so early, when he wanted to sleep? Why did I fuss at him about cleaning his room? Did I even acknowledge his wave when he started to the lake.?*

Before the rescue unit arrived, Marty's husband Carl found Jason's lifeless, pale, blue lipped body at the bottom of the lake in less than four feet of water. CPR was begun as a half crazed Julie cried to God, "Please, please God take me. Don't take my precious boy."

It was not to be. There was the funeral director, the overabundance of food, pastors, neighbors, friends, and Richard, all whirling like a blur through the distraught days that followed.

At long last, Julie was alone except for attentive, caring Richard. She was broken, a hollow shell, overwhelmed with grief. When the sedative induced fog wore off, she had to once again face the nightmare reality of that terrible day. *How can I go on? Why? Why*? Julie struggled back to work, back to church and tried her best to respond to Richard, who did everything possible to support and encourage her, seeing to her every need, but her heart had nothing left to give him. Her mind, her soul, her heart had been imprisoned, possessed by grief.

During dinner one night, sitting at the kitchen table with Richard, Julie picked at her food, knowing what she had to do. Head bowed, words came soft and whispery, "Richard, I am not the person you asked to marry you. I have been changed by this terrible thing that has happened."

"Stop, Julie. I won't listen to this. I love you. We are going to get through this together."

"No, Richard. I cannot be the wife you deserve. I want you to find someone who can make you happy, someone that makes you laugh. I will always be grateful for the love you have showed me and Jason, but I will not marry you."

The Tiger Yearbook was dedicated to Jason. A memorial bench was put in the school courtyard. Julie endured the ceremony with the support and help of Marty and Carl. She was appreciative, but these honors only intensified the reality of her loss.

Endless days passed and the heartache of life without Jason took more and more of a toll. Her appearance deteriorated.

She slept more and more as an escape, ate less and less. Tomorrow would be the second anniversary of Jason's death.

In an effort to keep her mind off Jason, Julie put on her walking shoes and started down the street. She thought about Marty telling her last week that Richard had moved back to Nebraska. She remembered the dreams she had for herself, Richard, and Jason. Mile after mile she walked until she was overtaken by exhaustion, her mind too numb to think.

The warm water felt soothing as she leaned back in the tub. She relaxed as she toweled off, put on her night clothes and climbed into a welcoming bed. A calmness about facing tomorrow surrounded Julie as she fell into coveted, peaceful sleep.

A bleakness hovered over Marty and Carl as they walked from the gravesite to their car. "Carl, do you believe someone can die from a broken heart? You know Dr. Bentley said the autopsy did not show a definitive cause of death for Julie"

Carl put his arm around Marty. "I don't know, Honey. I just don't know."

In the distance, a sky rocket from leftover fireworks was launched, spraying festive red, white and blue sparkles over two grave markers. One marker had the name Julie Lynch McCoy, January 11, 1949-July 4, 1989, LOVING MOTHER, and the other was lettered Jason Gregory McCoy, April 10, 1973-July 4, 1987, LOVING SON.

Ordinary Can Be Very Special

By Pam Baker

The barn of Sweet Willow Farm stands atop a grassy hill– the complete essence of rural charm. A barn is a barn, but this one is different. It looks like an illustration taken right out of a "Little Golden Book". It could not be more serene, more inviting, or more perfect. Beautifully symmetrical ancient oak trees frame the weathered, but freshly painted, red barn with its crossbuck doors. Clumps of yellow daffodils profusely bloom along the black board-fence that surrounds the picturesque barn.

Several black and white spotted cows contentedly chew their cud while lying in the shade of one of the majestic oaks. Two little calves frisk and romp among the older cows. Sitting framed in the doorway of the open barn door is a charcoal gray cat, licking her paw to groom herself. She is plump and healthy from her steady diet of mice that constantly try to steal the grain from the silo. If you look closely, you can see six of her little kittens happily playing on the bales of hay stacked high in the barn.

There is a dirt path bordered by wildflowers in a rainbow of colors, which meanders down to a small pond behind the barn. The pond is surrounded by willow trees dipping their long limber branches into the clear, calm water. The picture of serenity is completed by the soft, colorful chickens happily running through the wildflowers, searching for insects on their way to the pond to get a cool drink.

Those five hens came to Sweet Willow Farm as day-old chicks last spring, just one short year ago. They all looked quite different from one another when they arrived, and the difference now, as grown-up hens was even more striking.

Lily was a Black Australorp and her feathers were so black that in the sunlight they seemed to glisten with emerald greens and iridescent blues. And she laid such pretty eggs, a light brown color with dark brown speckles.

Roz was a Wellsummer chicken, and she looked quite regal. She had almost every shade of brown in her feathers. The soft feathers around her neck had gold and black in them, making it appear that she was wearing a lace collar. Her eggs were beautiful, too. They were such a dark brown that you could almost call them mahogany.

Daphne was an Araucana chicken. She had the soft coloration of a sweet Carolina Wren, and her eggs were blue. Blue!!!

Charlotte was a Rhode Island Red and her feathers were a deep russet color. They glistened with gold when the sun hit them just right. She laid eggs that were a soft creamy brown.

And then there was Miss White. When she came to Sweet Willow Farm with the other girls last spring, she felt special. When Miss White was a chick, she was a soft pastel yellow, almost like melted butter. She felt pretty. She doesn't feel pretty anymore; she feels as plain as plain can be. She was a White Leghorn, so, of course, she grew up to be a white chicken. And she laid plain white eggs. How boring. Even her name was boring. A white chicken who lays white eggs named Miss White–how dull can you get? Oh well. Walter, the farmer who cared for them, never seemed to favor one girl over the other, but Miss White couldn't help but feel a little inferior when she compared herself to the other hens.

But Miss White's problems right now were worse than her name and her feather and egg color. All the girls' egg production had lessened during the cold, dark winter months, but now that spring was here, everyone was back to giving Walter four, five, or six eggs each week. But Miss White had not recovered from the winter months–it had gotten worse. She hadn't laid a single egg in over two weeks! Miss White really liked Walter and couldn't help but feel that she was letting him down.

As the rest of the girls headed down to the pond, Miss White turned and slowly walked back to the barn. All the other hens had already done their work today and left an egg in the nesting box for Walter to collect–all but Miss White. Since it was not yet noon, Miss White thought she might go back to the nesting box and try again, but she was not hopeful. Something was not right. Her feathers had lost their luster shortly after Christmas and an alarming amount of them had fallen out. They were growing back now, but she felt plainer than ever. She entered the barn and went straight to her nesting box, hopped in, and sighed. No sooner had she settled in the box when Walter appeared with his egg basket. He was surprised to see Miss White in the barn all alone and asked her if anything was wrong. Of course, Miss White could not answer him back, but she gazed up at him with sorrowful eyes. Walter reached in the nesting box and pulled Miss White into his arms. While gently stroking the sad chicken's soft feathers, he began talking to Miss White.

"I think I know what is wrong," Walter said. "You are worried that your egg laying days might be over. Well, put that right out of your sweet little head. You've been molting lately, Miss White. It's a natural process, and it happens to all hens periodically. But don't worry, your feathers are growing back and soon you will look as beautiful as you ever did. And you will resume your egg laying duties in no time at all. That is the way it always has been, and there is no need to worry. Now run on down to the pond with the other girls and play. I know soon I'll be getting lots of pretty white eggs from my special Miss White," the farmer said as he placed the little hen on the ground.

Miss White was astonished! Walter had called her plain white feathers beautiful and said she was special! She clucked a "thank you" to Walter and, with great relief, scurried down the path to the pond.

The next day, Miss White woke early feeling strangely different. This is the day she just knew it. And sure enough, just as the sun was peeking over the horizon and illuminating the barn with soft morning light, Miss White produced a perfect white egg. She felt so proud!

Miss White hung around the barn all morning instead of going down to the pond with the other girls. She wanted to see Walter's reaction to the white egg.

"Why, Miss White, what a good girl you are!" Walter said as he reached into the nesting box. "I told you just yesterday that you would start giving me eggs again and you did it. You don't know how happy this makes me. The other girls have such colorful eggs, but at this time of year, your pretty white eggs are the ones that I want the most. Easter is a little over two weeks away and I am hoping you can give me a whole dozen of your beautiful white eggs by then. Yours are the only eggs I can dye for my Easter basket."

Miss White could hardly believe it. Even though the other girls laid such beautiful eggs, Walter wanted HERS most of all! She felt a little less plain and a little more special the rest of the day while she and the other girls played in the shade of the ancient oak trees.

One spring day blended into the next and all of the sudden, it was Good Friday. Miss White had completely recovered from her molting period and had now given Walter eleven eggs. Walter was so pleased with Miss White and had heaped words of praise upon her white feathered head. Miss White was very proud of herself, but had one more day and one egg to go. Could she do it?

Saturday dawned. A soft breeze whispered through the barn and gently ruffled Miss White's glistening feathers. While the other girls still slept, Miss White hopped up into the nesting box and made herself a comfortable nest in the fresh straw. She clucked softly as she waited. And just as the rising sun began to turn the dark sky to a soft pink, Miss White produced egg number twelve. Walter had wanted a dozen eggs and Miss White had made the wish come true. She could hardly wait until he came today to collect the eggs.

The other girls rose soon and took their turns in the nesting boxes. When everyone's work was done, they all scurried outside to search for bugs amid the daffodils and wildflowers. All but Miss White–she stayed behind to wait for Walter. When Miss White looked into the nesting box and saw the assortment of eggs, she was actually astonished to realize that her white egg looked just as pretty and special as all the colorful eggs. When Walter arrived to collect the eggs, the smile on his face was reward enough for Miss White. After gently placing all the eggs in the basket, Walter sat it down and reached for the little hen. Miss White dearly loved to be picked up and petted by the farmer. She was even more pleased when Walter began to speak as he gently stroked her soft feathers.

"Thank you so much, Miss White, for the beautiful eggs. I knew I could count on you!" Walter began. "Your eggs will be the crowning jewel in my Easter basket. You have made me very happy."

"Did I ever tell you how you got your name, Miss White?" Walter asked as he continued to stroke the little hen's soft back. "You probably think it is because you are a white chicken. Well, that is partly true. But there is another reason. There used to be a really good show on TV called 'The Wonder Years' that I just loved. One character on the show was a young, pretty English teacher and her name was Miss White. I liked that character so much that I named you after her."

Miss White could barely believe it. Her name that she had once thought plain and boring was actually very meaningful.

Walter set Miss White down and thanked her again for her part in making his Easter such a special day, then told her to go play and have fun with the other girls. With head held high and pride in her heart, she fairly sailed down the path between the beautiful wild flowers to join the other girls by the pond in the shade of the swaying willows.

Miss White never felt ordinary again. She felt special. She WAS special. Maybe her color appeared ordinary, and maybe her eggs were viewed as ordinary, and maybe her name sounded ordinary, but now Miss White knew better. Sometimes things that seem ordinary at first glance are, in reality, very special. And Easter forever remained Miss White's favorite holiday!

WE SHALL RETURN

By Linda Dye

The sun-drenched summer day sizzled, enveloping everything in its heat and humidity. The small town was preparing to celebrate the Fourth of July. Old Glory fluttered along Main Street in the steamy breeze and red, white and blue bunting, covering peeling paint, decorated the fronts of downtown stores in anticipation of the parade and fireworks on Friday. Independence Day is a big deal in small southern towns.

Georgia made her way along Main Street, on her way to Patterson's Drugstore to pick up a prescription, stopping to speak to a friend or neighbor, as is the custom in small towns, where people live and die in the family home on a street most likely bearing the family name. There is a familiarity and closeness that does not exist in city life, a security that Georgia needed at this point in her journey.

A car she recognized approached. It was Marie, Georgia's best friend since childhood. Marie and her husband Ben and Georgia and her husband Tom were close friends from the time of their teen marriages, on through to the years of celebrating the births of each other's grandchildren. Marie honked the horn, waved and rolled on down the street at a slow crawl.

After picking up her prescription, Georgia sat in the hot car, with the windows down, mesmerized and lulled by the Stars and Stripes swirling and flapping in the gentle breeze. Memories, like the festive fireworks to come, exploded in her mind of bygone Fourths, when the four friends would prepare to go on vacation to a small Florida island, discovered when they had attended a wedding in the vicinity.

Since that time, it became a twice a year ritual to head to the ocean for fun and relaxation. There were cheese straws and pound cake to be baked and carried along, enjoyed after lazy days spent on the beach, and four decks of cards for playing progressive rummy at night.

An important pattern was established in the lives of the four friends, their friendship deepening as the years went by, a stable, solid relationship that could be counted on in good times and hard times.

Spirits always ran high on the trips to the island, with much talk and laughter and a stop at their favorite restaurant discovery, where home cooking made mouths water and stomachs growl many miles before it was time to eat. Excitement intensified as they neared their destination.

The trips home, relaxed and tanned, gave time to reminisce about all the fun they had and plan for their return trip in a few short months. From the time of their first visit to the island, the crossing of the bridge connecting the island to the mainland was like a marker that ended the vacation, and the four would give a childlike shout, in unison, "We shall return," accompanied by claps, whistles and yells. It had become a ritual that symbolized a pact between the four.

And return they did, year after year. Twenty wonderful years of trips to the tropical paradise of sun and sand went by. The island was like a second home. Commercialism had passed it by and there had been few changes to the lazy, laid back surroundings over the years. It was their stomping ground. They knew every nook and cranny, all the places the locals ate, the best beach locations to look for shells. But nothing stays the same.

Georgia closed her eyes, resting her head on the head rest, thinking of their last trip to the island. Tom's health was fragile and failing. There was now a necessary wheelchair to be loaded into the car, bottles of medicine, too numerous to mention, and limitations that curtailed many activities, but the decision was made for the four friends to make the usual July Fourth trip, determined to have a good time.

Their first excursion on the island that July, led to a predicament that brought much laughter to the couples, as six hefty teenagers struggled and puffed in an effort to release Ben's new Cadillac, which had become stuck in the sand. He had been determined to drive onto the beach, since Tom's wheelchair would not allow him to be pushed in the deep sand. Apparently the Cadillac was not equipped to handle the sand either.

The three able-bodied friends were unhappy and unable to enjoy the beach without Tom's company, but continued to find ways to alter their usual activities to include Tom. Salt air, good food and sunshine always make everything better. Each new day was a gift to be enjoyed.

For many years, the women played the men in Rummy and Rook, always ending up the underdogs, until Marie and Georgia devised hand signals letting each other know which was their strong suite or what card they needed. It was on this trip that their cheating ways came to light, causing many disparaging, scolding remarks from the husbands. All the while, the wives had to endure comments from Ben and Tom that they had to let the wives win once in a while to keep them from resorting to cheating.

The final evening was spent at an upscale French restaurant where parking was scarce, requiring a long walk.

After the meal, a trip to the drugstore was made to replace Georgia's cosmetics that were lost when a large hole was worn in her straw purse, rubbing against the wheel of the wheelchair as she pushed Tom to the restaurant. Cosmetics were strewn for several blocks before it was noticed. The four shook their heads and covered their mouths as they looked at a trail left on the sidewalk from the spilled contents of Georgia's bag.

Like an omen, gray, rainy skies prevailed on the day of departure. A quick ride by of all their favorite spots was made, a deviation from the usual routine. The old shout of, "We shall return," as they crossed the bridge had a hollow ring to it. An unspoken truth hung heavy in the car and conversation lagged, with large gaps of silence.

"Georgia, Georgia." Georgia sprang to a sitting position, drenched in perspiration, when she heard Marie's voice. "Honey, are you okay? Do I need to drive you home? When I came back up the street looking for a parking place, things did not look right with you. What's wrong."

"Oh Marie, I must have fallen asleep. Can you imagine anyone doing that in this heat? I'm fine and will be heading home to cool off. Thanks for checking on me, dear friend. I do not know what I would have done without you and Ben these past few years."

On her drive home, Georgia enjoyed and appreciated the colorful decorations displayed in yards and on buildings, but to Georgia the Fourth of July would always be the four friends on the island, watching red, white and blue fireworks on the beach, eating their favorite yogurt, waving small flags, content and happy.

April Fool's Day

By Carolyn Bond

During the school year of 1923, my dad F. A. Johnson met my mother, Lucile Cleveland, at Centerville School in Elbert County GA. His name was Floyd Adolphus and he was called Adolphus. I wonder how often that name was made fun of, laughed at, and made the butt of jokes in the classroom? Especially because he had two brothers named "Bill" and "Pete!"

Their two families were not familiar with one another as his was a farming family who regularly share-cropped, and her family lived on her grandparents' acreage and her daddy was employed by Elbert County.

His family moved regularly, following places with housing available for a family of five children. Sometimes in South Carolina, North Carolina and back to Georgia, this time to Oglethorpe County, rather than Elbert County. There were three years' difference in their ages. How they became close is a mystery to me.

Her family moved to the city of Elberton in 1928. Her older sister had gone to work at the Silk Mill in Elberton and the family moved into one of the mill sponsored houses nearby. She would have been in the eleventh and final grade, at Centerville. By moving to town, she would have to repeat the tenth grade and graduate the following year. The family owned a Model T car and Lucile was allowed to drive that car back to Centerville School, so she could graduate with her class.

She found two people, one a teacher, who would ride with her, paying a small fee to help pay for gas. The six-mile drive was on a dirt road that was difficult to navigate when it rained.

The two kept in touch. He began working in one of the granite plants in Elberton. After graduation, she worked at Gallant-Belk Company when they established a store on the Elberton Square.

Their relationship was haphazard because he lived 20 miles away. But it flourished, and they became engaged to be married in 1933. They were married on April 1, 1934, at Bowman Baptist Church by her uncle Rev. A. J. Bussey, who was the pastor there.

They had a happy marriage and raised a son and two daughters. His favorite statement, when it came anniversary time, was always, “Yes, I sure was fooled on that April Fool’s Day.”

Erin Go Bragh

By Bonnie McAlarney

Artie Flynn from Killarney
Broad of face, full of blarney,
Says he knew St. Patty well
And helped him chase the snakes to Hell.

Across the town Bridey O'Neill
Who feeds the birds and wears a veil,
Writes pleasant verse and notes that rhyme
Inspired by St. Valentine.

Whether timid, whether loud,
All come along to join the crowd
That wear the green and play the harp
To dance the jig and celebrate . . .

Ireland Forever!

When You change the way you look at things, the things look at change.

-Wayne Dyer

Summer Beach Trip Contrast

By Linda Dye

Half-Empty Cup

Dark rain clouds loomed in the distance and Trey grimaced as he maneuvered the shiny new BMW along the narrow, seldom traveled, potholed road lined with unkempt, scraggly brambles. A twitchy feeling of apprehension and uneasiness gnawed at Beatrice, as she thought of the remoteness and isolation of the location. Rounding the curve, Beatrice and Trey let out a gasp that stuck in their throats as cottage 'Down the Hatch' came into view.

They had rented the cottage based on the recommendation of a friend. Trey pulled to a stop in front of a small, paint peeling, dilapidated cottage with one shutter askew and steps of warped, splintered boards leading to a swaying stoop adorned with a lone rusted lawn chair that had seen one too many storms. Access to the beach was an arduous trek over dunes infested with sandspurs and underbrush.

Beatrice slumped in her seat, pouty, sullen lips marring her pristine face. "Trey, I am heartsick. Just look at the condition of this place. There's no path to the beach. Can you imagine how horrible the inside must be?"

The interior was a throwback to the days of pine paneling, dark and depressing, casting a shadow of doom and gloom which was intensified by the approaching storm. A dank, musty smell emanated from every object, even the linens. As Beatrice and Trey made their way from one room to the next, cobwebs and accumulated dirt and dust stirred in their wake. Gazing out the kitchen window, goosebumps covered Beatrice's arms as she spotted a bird of prey feasting on an unidentifiable carcass.

The couple jumped and tightly clutched each other as a vibrant bolt of lightning cracked and sizzled, splitting through roiling clouds, and the front door was thrust open by a violent gust of wind. "Beatrice, Honey, it's not worth trying to stay here. This vacation is down the hatch." Giant raindrops pelted the desperate couple as they ran, stumbling down the wobbly steps, seeking the sanctuary of their shiny car eager to make a quick getaway.

Half-Full Cup

Dark rain clouds loomed in the distance as Joe maneuvered his jeep along the narrow, seldom traveled, potholed road lined with scraggly, unkempt brambles. Letty was filled with feelings of exhilaration and anticipation, relishing the solitude and privacy this location would offer. Rounding the curve, Letty and Joe let out a soft, "Oh my", as cottage, 'Beach Memories', came into view.

They had rented the cottage, sight unseen, because the price was within their budget. Joe pulled to a stop in front of a small, paint peeling, dilapidated cottage with one shutter askew and warped, splintered boards on steps climbing toward a swaying stoop adorned with a lone rusted lawn chair that had seen one too many storms. Access to the beach was an arduous trek over dunes infested with sandspurs and underbrush.

Letty danced and twirled, waving her arms in the air as she stepped from the jeep. "Joe, this is so quaint. Just our style. Can you imagine the hidden shell treasures buried in the dunes leading to the beach and the adventures we will have exploring them?"

The interior's dark, throwback pine paneling and the dank, musty smell permeating everything, including linens, set Joe and Letty in motion. They flung windows wide open, letting the wonderful salt air flow throughout, dispelling any hint of mustiness. Letty placed bright citrus colored beach towels across the backs of chairs, giving the rooms a sunny, cherry feeling, and an assortment of fruit was placed in a cracked bowl, adding charm to the kitchen. Letty smiled and called to Joe as she spied a pair of rabbits contentedly nibbling grass at the backdoor.

A blanket and a glass of Chardonnay in hand, Joe and Letty headed for the stoop, where they lay watching the pelting rain and listening to the noisy gulls as they sipped the dry wine and expounded on their good fortune at finding cottage, 'Beach Memories', and how the week ahead would be a time to unwind and enjoy the simpler things of life.

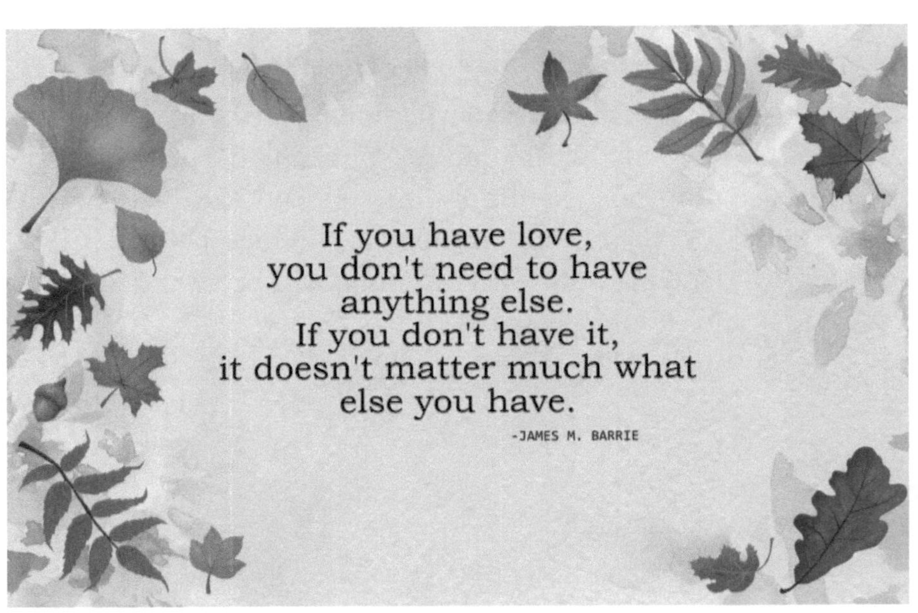
If you have love,
you don't need to have
anything else.
If you don't have it,
it doesn't matter much what
else you have.
-JAMES M. BARRIE

A Patchwork Thanksgiving

By Pam Baker

Although Helen had never lived anywhere else in her 19 years on this earth, she didn't think there could be a better place in the whole world than Virginia's Shenandoah Valley. The peaceful valley was bounded by the beautiful Allegheny Mountains to the west and the lovely Blue Ridge Mountains to the east. Something about being nestled between these two majestic forces of nature made Helen feel safe, like she was being gently held in a secure nest.

It was a gorgeous Friday afternoon in September as Helen, despite being tired and sore from a very long day of picking apples at Sunny Ridge Orchard, walked past the rustic farm houses on her way back to town and home to her Harry. She and Harry had already been married over a year, but she still felt like a blushing bride when she thought of him. She smiled to herself, picturing the pleasure on Harry's face when she handed him her wages from the past few weeks of picking apples. Today the job was finished and all the apples had been picked and crated. The orchard owner had been so pleased with her work that he had given her a $2 bonus. Two whole dollars—Helen couldn't believe it! This would go a long way in easing the young couple's financial worries.

The great depression had been devastating America for three years now and so many had lost their jobs and had nowhere to turn. The poor Midwest had been subject to drought and windstorms, and so many of those unfortunate people had lost everything. Here in Virginia, the weather had been kinder, probably thanks to those beautiful mountains that sheltered her beloved valley. Helen had been taking in washing and ironing, working in the peach orchards in the springtime and the apple orchards in the fall. Harry was lucky to still have his job at Simpson's General Store. Compared to so many others, they were doing quite well. Things could be better, of course, but they could definitely be worse, and Helen counted her blessings daily.

She decided she would splurge a little today and stopped at the butcher shop on the way home to pick up a couple of pork chops for supper. Pork chops were Harry's favorite and he would be so pleased! They were 20¢ a pound, but Helen threw caution to the wind and bought them, anyway. Ham was up to 38¢ a pound, but Helen thought she might be able to pick up a small slice for under a quarter. It would be a double bonus—ham to go with the bean soup she had planned for Saturday's supper and she'd save a little to go with their eggs on Sunday morning. Meat for all three days of the weekend—what a rare treat!

Helen busied herself in her small kitchen in the little bungalow that she and Harry rented. The rent was a little high–$12.50 a month–but as long as Helen could supplement Harry's income with her washing, ironing, and seasonal farm work, the couple would be alright. The pork chops were sizzling on the stove and had filled the small home with a lovely aroma when Harry opened the back door and stepped into their home. Helen noticed he seemed a little less cheerful than usual, but his face brightened as he watched Helen deftly turn the chops over. He walked up behind her and wrapped his arms around her slim waist, kissing her on top of her head.

Helen dished up supper and the young couple sat in their kitchen eating their meal while quietly talking over the events of their day. Harry praised the pork chops, but didn't seem as thrilled with the special meal as Helen had expected. That worried her. While they stood side by side at the sink, Helen washing and Harry drying, she found out the reason for Harry's preoccupation during the meal.

He had been told today that due to the hard times, his hours were going to be cut in half. As bad as that sounded at the time, Harry was grateful that he still had a job. He reassured Helen that he would take care of things and everything would be okay. He optimistically told her he would now have half the week available to look for odd jobs and construction projects and that they would be fine.

Helen knew Harry would try his very best, but she also knew that there was very little work out there to be had. This was not good, not good at all. In fact, it was horrible. There would be no way they could maintain their life as it now was without Harry's full paycheck. She knew a lot of young couples who had fallen on hard times and were forced to move back in with their folks. As hard as it would have been to give up their privacy and independence, this would not be an option for Helen and Harry. Both Helen's parents had died during the pandemic of 1919 and she had been raised by her sweet grandmother, who was now also gone. Harry's parents lived far away and were barely getting by. Helen and Harry were on their own.

Throughout October, the young couple worked as hard as they could, trying their best to find ways to pick up some extra income. Helen managed to add a few more washing and ironing customers, and Harry found a few odd jobs here and there. But times being as they were, hardly anyone had much cash. Sometimes, Helen ended up trading her services for a dozen eggs or a young chicken to fry. Harry's endeavors brought a little bit of cash, but more often for his day's work, he came home in the evening with an armload of firewood for their kitchen stove or a bucket of coal for the pot-bellied stove that heated their home. But these trades helped the couple immensely. The less they had to spend on food and fuel, the more money it freed up to pay for things that required cash. At the end of the month, they spread their meager savings out on the kitchen table and were thankful that there was actually enough cash to meet the next month's obligations.

This continued into November, but by mid-month, the young couple had to admit that unless something changed soon, they were going to lose their little bungalow and would have to seriously begin searching for a more humble place to live. But where? There were few options and none were desirable.

And just when things seemed the darkest, a golden opportunity dropped into Harry's lap. On the Friday before Thanksgiving, one of Harry's elderly firewood customers made him a fantastic proposal. Mrs. Harris had tragically lost her husband a few years ago and without a man to take care of the small projects as they arose, the house began to fall into disrepair. And to add insult to injury, the cold weather had made Mrs. Harris's arthritis so much worse that there was no way she could make it through the winter months without help–help she could not afford.

She made the offer to Harry that he and Helen could move into the little summer kitchen on the back of the property rent free in exchange for Harry helping out some with the repairs and firewood chores and Helen preparing the evening meal for her. This was wonderful news for Harry and, hoping that Helen would approve, he accepted the offer on the spot.

Before starting for home, Harry walked the short distance to the little summer kitchen to see what he had gotten himself into. It was a one room structure that was built just as soundly as the big farmhouse. It had a stove that could serve both for cooking and heating and a big sink compete with a hand pump–no carrying water! There were shelves for dishes and foodstuffs, a small table with two chairs and a trapdoor in the floor that opened to reveal a small underground cold storage chamber. There was enough room left for their double bed and a couch. It would be a tight fit, but it could work. The bad news was that even though the little cabin seemed like a snug place to spend the winter, it was very dirty and very drab. But Helen had told him on many occasions that as long as she could go to sleep in his arms and wake up beside him, she would be happy. Well, the truth of that statement was going to be tested soon.

Harry was both excited and dreading telling Helen his big news. He decided that instead of telling her, he would show her. When he got home that evening, he told Helen that tomorrow morning he had a surprise for her and she could not ask questions. On Saturday morning after breakfast was over and the dishes cleared, washed and put away, they both put on their coats and hats. Harry grabbed Helen's gloved hand and off they went. Helen could not imagine what Harry was up to, but if he thought this was something good, then it definitely would be.

They turned into Mrs. Harris's farmhouse lane and Helen was surprised when they passed by the house and kept on going. What in the world? As they approached the summer kitchen, Harry feared that this was a really bad idea, but because there was truly no alternative, there was no turning back now. Harry opened the door and ushered Helen into the cramped quarters. He watched her face closely, so afraid that he would see revulsion and disgust. He could not believe it when Helen's face broke into a huge smile and she joyfully threw her arms around him. She saw the drabness, and she saw the dirt, but she also saw the wonderful possibilities. She told him it would be their own little heaven here on earth and she would make it into a cozy home for them–just give her a few days.

It was with great relief they spent that weekend, Harry trying to figure out how to haul their meager belongings to the little summer kitchen, and Helen with her own plans that she chose not to share with Harry. Now it was her turn to tell Harry that he could ask no questions!

Helen spent the first three days of the following week at their new "home", scrubbing and scouring and preparing her surprise. It took a lot of imagination and even more work, but when she closed the summer kitchen door to return to their little bungalow on Wednesday afternoon, she was quite pleased with the results of all her hard work.

Thanksgiving dawned, and Helen woke early to begin her dinner preparations. She had scrimped and saved and traded her way to what she thought would be a glorious meal. When the little hen was baked to perfection, instead of placing the meal on the table, she loaded everything into a cardboard box and told Harry to grab his coat. A few moments later, a dumbfounded Harry was carrying their Thanksgiving dinner down the street, following a giggling Helen.

They walked the short distance to the summer kitchen and when Helen opened the door to it, Harry could not believe his eyes. What a transformation! It was sparkling clean and everything fairly glistened. Mrs. Harris had supplied some leftover paint, stain, and varnish, and Helen had painted the shelves and refinished the table and chairs. The floor had been scrubbed with sand and water and was smooth and glossy. But the biggest and best surprise was the walls. Helen had acquired an outdated wallpaper sample book from the hardware store and had papered the entire room with the pretty swatches. Harry felt like he was wrapped in a giant patchwork quilt! There they ate their simple meal, surrounded by the comfort and tranquility those four walls provided, completely happy and truly thankful.

The years passed and prosperous times returned. Helen and Harry spent many more Thanksgivings together throughout their long and happy life. But that Thanksgiving, their Patchwork Thanksgiving, forever remained their favorite–the year when they had nothing, but they had it all.

Holiday Home Ladies Celebrate Halloween

By Ann Davis

Kelly and David made the long trip from their home to the retirement center that her Mom moved into recently. Kelly's family home was selling soon, so they were moving out some of the furniture to take back to their home. Kelly had tried to prepare David for the change in her Mom. David had only known her as Betty, a sensible down-to-earth woman who had hardly varied her daily routine as long as he had known her. He was sure that Kelly was exaggerating about this new "Mom" called Liz. He was very aware that Kelly and her Mother were not always "on the same page" to say the least. But in his mind, no one could change that much.

They arrived at Liz's small bungalow home to find a note on the door, "Kelly, come to the game room. Our costumes came today."

Kelly turned to David, "You are coming too, now you will see."

They could hear shrieks and laughter before they got near the game room. Looking in, they saw boxes, bags and cartons covering the floor and tables of the room. Women of all shapes and sizes were pulling out bright-colored clothes. There were feather boas, large & small hats, gloves, petticoats, high heels in all sizes, and at least two of what appeared to be big hoops for dresses.

"Good heavens, what have they done now?" Kelly said to herself. She was sure that David (a quiet, reserved man) was in total shock. However, turning to look at him, she got a surprise. David had a big smile on his face. "Let's go find Liz," he said.

Liz was in the middle of the room, pulling out more loot from the boxes. "I found the wraps," she yelled, though no one could hear her above the din.

She grabbed David and Kelly in a bear hug when she saw them. "You're just in time to help us with the dresses." Today she was dressed in stylishly torn jeans and a tee shirt that said, "I LIVE TO BOOGIE." Her feet were bare, but her toenails were painted bright blue. Once again, Kelly could only stare in surprise. "Well, what is it, Kelly? You don't expect me to wear my good clothes to unpack, do you? My sandals are around here somewhere." David was still absorbing the activity going on all around him. Liz took charge of the situation. "Why don't the two of you go on to my place and unpack your stuff? I'll be on in just a bit. We have to separate things out here so that we can get this room cleared out a little. Go on now."

Kelly and David went back to the cottage in silence. However, as soon as they shut the door to the cottage, Kelly exploded. "Did you see that? She looks like an over age hippie. What is she thinking?"

David hung up their clothes. Kelly fumed. "Well, say something."

"Okay, I think your Mother is having fun. What is the harm?" David answered. "She doesn't seem to be hurting anyone. They all looked pretty happy to me. Let's just wait and see what happens. If they start to make voodoo dolls or sacrifice male virgins, we can step in. I don't really think they'll find any male virgins, so we shouldn't have to worry." As usual, he made Kelly laugh, and she had to cheer up.

After Liz came, they went out to dinner. She spent the meal time telling them about the plans for the big Halloween costume bash coming up soon. "I know you have to pack up and move the furniture tomorrow, but I want you to come the very next day. We will be getting ready for the party that day." Kelly promised to get there in time to help where she could.

After packing up what they could the following day, they slept in the next day and rested. They arrived in the game room shortly after lunch. A fashion parade appeared to be in progress, accompanied by loud hoots, laughter and comments, some rather "catty and sharp." No one seemed to take offence.

David sat down by a stout woman with gray "helmet hair" that appeared to stay in place no matter what happened to her. She introduced herself as Ethel. "Don't pay attention to what all these old broads are saying. Some of them ain't the sharpest tools in the shed even on their best days. Right now, they just plain crazy."

Just then, a small woman entered the room. She was wearing a blue cowgirl outfit trimmed out with white fringe and a white fancy western hat to match. Her hair was very large and very blonde. She had a small waist and a large bust. She had a small rope lasso in her hand. "That there's Bobbie. She's going to the dance as Dolly Parton. I reckon you figured that out for yourself." Ethel said to David. "She used to do hair. She's been doing the hairstyles for some of the girls. They all look just alike, great big teased up hair that wouldn't move in a tornado. No way would I let her touch mine. I still got some sense left myself." David just looked on in great amusement as two more Dollies came through, each one brighter, blonder and more bosomy than the last.

There was a slight commotion near the door where several women waited in the hall to be announced. Liz had decided that the ladies needed introducing. "Good grief, Liz, just bring 'em on in. Don't you think we know who all these wrinkled old prunes are anyway? Wigs and makeup can't hide some things." Ethel yelled.

"Oh hush up, Ethel. You need to go get your hormone shot. You're getting grouchy." Liz shouted back.

Liz announced the next group. "Next we have Princess Leia. Tonight she will be accompanied by Luke Skywalker."

"Whooee!" Ethel hollered out. "Give me that Han Solo. He wouldn't have to be Solo for long with me around." By now, David was trying not to fall off the couch laughing. He had spotted Kelly out in the hall with a group of ladies. She was frantically adjusting wigs, hats, and applying makeup on anyone left with a dab of natural skin showing.

Three Princess Leia's entered together. The first one was close to six feet tall. She wore the white robe with braided hair that looked like fat pancakes at her ears. The next one wore battle gear complete with plastic weapon. She appeared to be about four and a half feet tall. David thought he would be far more frightened of the amazon in white. The last one was quite original. She wore a filmy veil cover from her neck to her ankles. Underneath appeared to be a rather large gold two piece swim suit cut to cover far more than the usual suit. She wore a gold head piece. This unusual Princess was on the large side of the scale weighing over 175 lbs.

"How'd they get enough gold cloth to cover you up, Eunice? You gonna need more'n that little thin sheet to cover you up tonight! Why didn't you go as Chewbacca? You got enough body hair to look natural." Ethel hollered at Eunice.

Eunice just turned to look at Ethel. "Well, at least I can get in a costume. They ain't making em' big enough for you!" she said with a little sneer.

"Now girls, let's be nice. We all have our little age areas that we want to cover. That's normal for middle-aged ladies like ourselves." Liz said.

"Middle aged! Liz, there ain't nobody here can remember middle age much less be it." Ethel said, loud enough for all to hear. Some ladies "booed" Ethel.

The parade of women in costumes continued. There was great variety in the lineup of subjects. There were two Cleopatras, one Scarlet O'Hara, one Annie Oakley, complete with pistols in holsters that kept sliding down to her knees, as she was quite thin. Next, a witch wearing a tall black hat, a very large ballerina complete with pink tights and a tutu. That brought hoots and catcalls from several of the ladies. Then a fairy godmother in sparkling costume swooped in complete with her magic wand.

Helen yelled to her, "Margie, you gonna turn some of these old broads into princes tonight? I don't see no men here."

"She's gonna turn them into frogs." Ethel yelled back. That brought more boos from the ladies.

Last but not least was Liz as Wonder Woman. She had on a short skirt, a headpiece with a star, and a cape. But what really grabbed the attention was the gold and red top part of the costume. It covered the generous bosom part of Liz's anatomy. Liz swirled her cape out with great fanfare. She was greeted with cheers and laughter.

"Oh, good grief! What next?" Kelley said to David. He appeared to be in shock.

The ladies all paraded back into the room with great fanfare and noise. Costumes were checked for any fabric rips or tears, as some were stretched rather tight. No one wanted a surprise during the festivities that evening.

Kelley & David found Liz amid the noise and confusion. They were going back to their motel to rest and have dinner. Liz asked, “Aren’t you coming to the party? We’re going to have some fun. We have asked all the men who live at the Veteran’s Home to come. They’ve accepted our invitation. It should be lots of fun. We have a DJ coming too.”

Kelley just stared at Liz. David answered for both of them. “Oh yeah, we’re coming. We wouldn’t miss it for the world.”

As they walked to the car, Kelley said, “Are you crazy? Do you have any idea what those weird old women may do tonight?”

“No, I don’t. But I want to watch and see for myself. It should be good.”

THE PARTY

David & Kelley ate a quick dinner before putting on their costumes. Liz insisted they had to wear something festive to fit the occasion. Kelley had looked in the closets at her Mom’s house. She found an old leisure suit with bright flowered shirt that was her Dad’s. It fit David reasonably well. She came up with a bright, short, shapeless dress from her teen years. They would go as a couple from the 70s. That would have to do for the evening.

They were surprised to see several large vans, cars, and one small bus at the Elks club hall that had been rented for the occasion. Apparently, this was a large group affair that included all the personal care homes in the area. Upon entering, they saw tables and chairs set up on one side of the room, an area for dancing was on the other side. Dinner was just finishing up and people were moving from table to table, talking and laughing. There were three tables full of only men. Some of them were wearing military uniforms from all the branches of the military. From the style and fit of the uniforms, these were from years past. These veterans had decided that ladies could not resist a “man in uniform." From the looks the ladies were giving them, it appeared to be true. Liz stood and waved to David and Kelley to come and sit at her table. They made their way through tables of ladies in every style of costume. There were fairy tale characters from Little Red Riding Hood to Little Bo Peep. Red was wearing long blonde pig tales and carried a basket. She appeared to be more the age of Grandma in the story, but she was unfazed by this idea. Bo Peep wore a peek-a-boo blouse complete with push-up under garments. She had a large toy sheep by her chair and a long shepherd's staff with a crook at the end. David immediately saw the possibility of some veteran being pulled in by the staff. He gave her table a wide space as he moved through the room.

There were at least six Dolly Parton look-a-likes. They ranged in size from under five feet tall to almost six feet tall. Of course, all of them had bosoms that rivaled the real lady herself. Two thin ladies looked to be in danger of toppling over on their face. Only one or two of the ladies were wearing the high heels that Dolly is famous for wearing. The other ladies had conceded to age and wore shoes with low heels. One lady had on her black orthopedic shoes with thick soles. She did not seem bothered that they did not quite match up with the blue fringed cowgirl skirt and shirt she wore. The outfit was completed with a white cowboy hat perched on the large bouffant wig on her head.

As they sat down, a very tall lady rose to take the microphone for a short welcome to the group. It was hard to miss her costume choice as the Statue of Liberty. She carried her torch above her head as though she were lighting her way. Miss Liberty welcomed everyone, and thanked everyone who had helped plan and prepare for the evening. She reminded everyone to be aware of medications and overuse of the punch tonight. "We don't want to have another 'Incident' tonight." At the mention of the "Incident" there were soft murmurs throughout the room. Several of the men laughed and clapped each other on the shoulder. One table of ladies just looked at their plates and sat quietly.

One woman from The First Baptist Church table stood up to get Miss Liberty's attention. "The punch will be just punch tonight. We voted on it; remember?"

"You are correct, Muriel. I had forgotten." Miss Liberty replied. "Who is in charge of the punch tonight?" she asked?

A lady from the First Presbyterian Church table replied, "The Holiday Home group."

All eyes turned to the tables of The Holiday Home group. Liz smiled serenely and nodded to the other tables.

"What happened?" Kelley asked Liz.

Several of the ladies stared at Liz with great concern. "Now dear, we don't break our promises here at the home. No need to talk about our past little indiscretions." You could hear an audible sigh of relief around the table.

About that time, the DJ started the music, and the tension in the room quickly faded. As usual, the dancing started slowly. Some of the more daring ladies stood and sway to the music alone. Gradually, others joined. Some veterans asked the ladies to dance. As the music moved to a slower song; all the Dolly's in the room were asked to dance. David found it interesting that some of the Dolly's could hardly stand upright with the extra bosoms pulling them forward. But the men were unfazed; they just held them tight enough to help them stand straight. As time went on, the music grew louder, the dancing more energetic. More and more people danced, alone, with a partner, or in a group. David and Kelley joined the dancers, enjoying the festivities. After a fast, active dance, David went to get them a cup of punch. He turned the cup up to drain it in one gulp. His face turned red. He coughed and took a breath. He quickly shook his head at Kelley as she raised her cup to drink. No doubt about it, someone had spiked the punch.

During a break in the music, David joined the veterans at the adjoining table. He had noticed a flask move around the table so that each man could add to the cup in front of him. David was very curious about the "Incident." He thought it was a good bet that at least one man would be happy to talk about it. Since David was a Navy veteran himself, he picked a Navy vet who introduced himself as Steve; to spend some time with first. After some brief time discussing past active duty, David brought up his question. "So what happened here last year? What's the big secret?"

Steve looked around the table and lowered his voice. "Some of the group got bored with the dancing last year. Eight or ten people moved into one of the rooms to play cards. You know hearts, or some usual game. They had a couple of tables going back there."

"Well, that sounds pretty tame to me. No big deal about that."

"There wouldn't have been a big deal, except that someone got the bright idea to play poker. They started playing poker for toothpicks."

"I guess some people might consider that gambling and object." David replied. "Doesn't seem too terrible to me."

"Well, it wouldn't have been a problem, but after a while some clothes came off the players." Steve told him as he tried to suppress a laugh.

"You mean they were playing strip poker?" David whispered in disbelief.

"Yep, they sure were. The men were losing, too. Shoes and socks went first, then ties, watches, rings, coats, shirts, a couple of toupees. The ladies had more extras to take off. First the jewelry, necklaces, bracelets, earrings, hair clips, a few rings, shoes. A couple of them peeled right out of their thigh high hose. At least three ladies had come out of their blouses, but they had their slips under that, so they were still covered. One lady just had on a half-slip, so she was a little more exposed. They say it was getting really interesting when Liz and some of the other Happy Home ladies walked in the room."

"Why," asked David, "what happened."

"That Happy Home lady with the gray helmet hair made a move on old Lester."

"You mean Ethel?" David asked with shock.

"That's the one. She said that Lester had to take his pants off. Lester had taken off everything, including his partial plate. The pants were next. Lester balked at that. So Ethel was ready to give him a hand with the pants. About that time, Liz and some of the other ladies and a few of the men came into the room. I thought they might have a stroke." He laughed again, remembering the shock on the faces of the group coming in to see eight half naked old folks sitting at the tables.

"What happened next?" David asked.

"They had to find their clothes and get back in them. That takes a while when you get older. I guess it's difficult to get into thigh high hose when you are past seventy years old. Then the party broke up. You can't keep a thing like that a secret. By the time we all got back to our houses, everyone knew about it." Steve told him.

David moved back to the table with Kelley. "You aren't going to believe what I just heard." He told Kelley.

But Kelley wasn't listening. She was watching as two or three brown paper bags were passed around the table. The ladies would look in the bag and keep it or pass it on. She had observed the same thing happening at the other tables. When the bag got almost to her, they passed it back the other way. She moved around to talk to Liz. "What in the heck is going on here? Are they passing booze?" Kelley asked Liz.

"Oh no, dear." Liz replied. "They are exchanging books. Most of the books are somewhat naughty, so we put them in bags, so some of the ladies are not embarrassed."

Kelley shook her head in disbelief. "You're not embarrassed to read them, but you don't want anyone to know you're reading them?"

"That's right, dear. We try to be sensitive to other's feelings." Liz replied.

Kelley looked at David. "Wait until I tell you about the paper bags." She told him.

About then the music started again. By now, everyone had sampled the spiked punch. Some of the ladies were pretty happy. The ladies from The First Baptist Church table appeared to be thrilled by now. None of them had danced at first, but now all were up dancing. Some were rather uninhibited in their movements. David looked around the room; most all the Church ladies from the Presbyterian, Episcopal and Methodist tables were dancing. As the boisterous laughing and dancing grew louder, someone turned up the music. It seemed the crowd got even louder to compensate. Only a few people remained seated at the tables. They were content with watching the dancers. Some were sipping punch. Several ladies had pulled the books out of the brown paper bags and were engrossed in reading the torrid paperback books. David observed the focused looks on their faces. He wondered if they would have heard a tornado alert siren at that moment.

The dancers were in full swing by now. Some were sipping punch while they danced alone or with a partner. Shoes had been discarded. Two Dolly wigs had been transferred to heads that had been bald for over thirty years. The men were wearing them proudly while they swung their partners. The ladies looked a little strange with their gray hair shining over the extra-large bosoms. They did not appear the least bit embarrassed.

Just when Kelley and David thought the music and action could not get louder, someone turned it up a notch. Feet moved faster, and skirts swung out wider.

"There's going to be some sore muscles and sore feet tomorrow." David shouted to Kelley. He had to shout to get his voice over the music and general hilarity of the crowd.

Just then, the doors of the hall burst open. A tall, stern man in his stiff blue uniform marched in. He moved into the room, other officers followed, spreading out into the room. The dancers kept dancing, unaware of the change. The readers did not look up at all.

David tried to pull Kelley aside into a small alcove; he had a bad feeling about this change. But Kelley was rooted to her spot by the punch bowl.

The tall man put a bullhorn to his mouth. "This is a raid!"

At the announcement, someone lowered the volume on the music. But some dancers kept moving anyway. Gradually, a change in atmosphere moved over the room. The ladies and veterans moved back to their tables. The Dolly wigs were sheepishly removed from the bald heads and returned to their owners. The naughty books were slipped into paper bags and slipped into purses. An uneasy hush fell over the room.

The tall officer with the bull horn appeared to be in charge. He moved toward the front of the room. The group from the Holiday Home sat silent and still. Ethel had her back to the door, so she was unaware of the officer. As he turned to face the room, he saw Ethel. She turned to her friend next to her asking loudly, "What the heck is going on? Who stopped the party?" Just then, she saw the tall officer standing at the front of the hall.

"Well, what the hell are you doing here, Eugene?" she shouted. "I thought you were coming to see me Sunday."

Eugene's face colored bright red. The other policeman looked dismayed. Some shuffled their feet and tried to back closer to the doors. They were wondering what to do now. So was Eugene.

One of the ladies engrossed in her naughty book looked up and shouted, "Well, it's Ethel's little Eugene. Hey there, Eugene, how's it going?"

Ethel had moved to the front by Eugene. "Hello there, son! Glad to see you. I thought I would see you Sunday."

The other ladies got up to give Eugene a hug. By now, the other policemen were at a total loss as to what they were supposed to do now. They looked at each other and shrugged. Eugene struggled to regain dignity and control. It was quite difficult with a group of ladies in wild costumes crowding around him. Finally, he regained some control and moved to speak to the microphone to speak to the group.

"We had some complaints about the loud music and laughing coming from this building tonight. We're asking you to go on home now. It's late and we don't want the neighbors making formal complaints about you. Just get your belongings together and go home."

The group reluctantly got their things together. There was some muttering about not being able to have a good time anymore, but they moved toward the doors. Eugene gave a big sigh of relief.

People said their goodbyes with hugs and handshakes. It took some time to gather up all the extra wigs, shoes and other odd belongings that a party generates. Liz moved to the microphone one more time. "Attention, attention, everyone. Remember our Thanksgiving party the Saturday after Thanksgiving. This year the veterans are going to be the pilgrims and we're going to be the Indians. We are going to have a wonderful time. Get your costumes ready. We will let you know who is in charge of the punch. Bye, bye now!!

Eugene sat down on the nearest chair and started shaking his head. He was muttering, "Pilgrims and Indians. Good grief, I'm going to have to call in extra officers for that thing. How am I going to explain that to the chief? How much longer can people that age keep this up?"

David walked over to pat his shoulder. "Don't you hope that you're doing this stuff when you're that age? I wouldn't miss that Thanksgiving party for all the turkey you can eat."

"I'm putting in for my vacation that week. If I'm coming to the party, I'm getting myself a Pilgrim outfit."

Raising his bullhorn, he shouted, "Load up, guys. We're done here. At least until right after Thanksgiving."

The Big Catch

By Robert Vasvary

They all were to gather at the Rocky Bottom bar that Friday evening for the Captain's meeting of the big 1st Annual Fishing Tournament that started bright and early the next morning. Being that it was a holiday weekend, this added to the excitement. Spring Break was in full effect and with Saint Paddy's day having just passed, everyone was reeling in vacation mode. This was the last weekend of the break. Everyone was there and on time, including our Captain Keene. They were all pumped and thirsty, which was not necessarily a good thing. They all needed to get up early if we wanted to catch that prize winning fish.

The plan for the tournament and rules were laid out formally by the owner of the bar and tournament sponsor. After that, everyone started drinking and carrying on like any other Friday night. The Captain and some of the other cohorts that were on his boat said they were heading to the Avenue and suggested that Jim should join them. Jim knew better and declined. He wanted to be ready to catch that prize fish off of Captain Keene's boat, which he had impulsively named, "The Hookers." Drunk Joe was fully convinced to join them for a few drinks, but Jim talked him out of it. Before the captain left for the Avenue, Jim and Joe had paid their $100 entry fee and were to meet at the dock at 6:00 am. Everyone else paid their entry fees to the bar or their captain. It was on!

After the others left for the Avenue, Jim worked hard to make sure he didn't lose Drunk Joe and insisted he crash at his house so there were no disconnects the next morning if he was going to be at the boat… on time. Joe agreed, and they proceeded with their Friday night drinking and karaoke fun, foregoing a trip downtown. The roadhouse was cranking, and the booze was flowing. There was so much fun to be had that Jim and Drunk Joe quickly lost track of time. Joe had agreed to crash at Jim's place and they agreed to leave the bar early (1AM was usually early for them). They were to stop on the way home for plenty of beer and ice and go back to quickly pack the coolers and have everything they needed securely in the car so they would not be late for the early morning muster at the Captain's boat at 7AM!

Around 5:30AM when Jim's alarm went off, he rolled over and immediately hit the snooze, still reeling from the booze in his head. After pushing the snooze button three times, he awoke with a shock of fear he had already missed muster. Before waking Joe, he tried calling the captain to make sure he was awake. He got nothing but voicemail! Jim tried texting several times, went downstairs for a glass of water came back up and then laid back down for a quick 20 minute snooze.

He awoke again, what seemed seconds later to see that the clock showed 7:05AM. He jumped out of bed and ran to the guest room, and shook Joe.

"Wake up man, we are late and I cannot reach the captain!"

Joe awoke after shaking him several times, and it took him a minute to get his senses together.

From there, it was a blur. They made their way to the garage and Jim was, at first, not sure if they had even stopped at the store on the way home for necessary supplies.

What time had we left the bar? Jim thought in his panic.

They literally stumbled to the garage. They had made a stop, but all they picked up was beer from a local store that was open late. Jim couldn't even remember what time they got home. Of course, they hadn't even packed in advance. They quickly loaded the car with whatever they could muster and speeded over to the Captain's house.

Jim knocked on Captain Keene's door several times and there was no answer. In his current state, all Jim could do was start dialing. He was frantic with the thought that we had missed the boat. At this point, in his relations with the patrons of this new world pirate bar (the place was built in the early 1940s) there was no way in hell he wanted to miss out on this huge holiday event.

He tried calling the other crew members and got nothing. Jim was about to bang on the door one last time and the door flew open. There stood the Captain, eyes half open and swaying in the doorway. He obviously had over-indulged the night before as well.

Jim looked over at Joe, who was slowly coming around. Jim's head was banging by now but the feeling was instantly replaced with a renewed spirit of adventure and zest for the day!

"Captain, wake your ass up! We have a tournament to win," he growled.

Douglas Keene was one of the best fisherman he had met since he started learning the ways of the seas on the South Florida Coast. He had his own marine repair business and was quite successful at it. He could find, fix and flip anything nautical and was a whiz at tinkering with any engine. He was not, however, the best Captain. He always relied on his scallywag cohort Jamaica Bob, who was quite the character. Bob didn't drink, but had more vices to make up for that, especially working deals and shady ones at that. He always took the helm once the captain started drinking. At least the Captain was smart enough to relinquish his boat to his trusted co-captain. As for the other boats, there was much competition for today's tournament and Jim recalled, not so vividly at this moment, that Captain Veroni had left the bar only an hour after the rest of the boatsmen had left for the Avenue. He was sure the other crafts were in the water by now and had already started heading 15 miles into the great Atlantic Ocean to where the Mahi and Black Fin Tuna were running this time of year.

Keene rubbed his eyes and tried to focus as he gained consciousness. It came to no surprise to Jim that there was no sense of urgency, as he was sure the captain had stayed out most of the night. From inside, he could hear someone making coffee.

"Come around back to the Tiki bar whilst I gather my things and we can head to our boats together. Not to worry, I know where the fish are and no one else knows my spot," he mumbled confidently while rubbing his eyes.

That wasn't enough for Jim. He didn't know that spot and was still a bit of a rookie. This was his first tournament, and it was not off to a great start. His anxiety was through the roof. He had been looking forward to this day since the announcement of the 1st Annual Rocky Bottom bar's tournament a month ago. He looked over at Joe, who was swaying in the morning breeze. The sun was making its way over the palm trees and the weather this morning was perfect. It was about 75 degrees and humid with a slight breeze that whispered of calm seas just a few miles away off the coast.

Jim nudged Joe in the backyard's direction and they made their way around to the Tiki bar. They both took a seat and Jim rubbed his eyes. His head was banging by now and he was ready to eat something to keep from throwing up. He had some chips he had grabbed from the car and was trying to get them down to dry up the rum and cokes he had been tossing down just hours ago.

"What time did we leave the bar," asked Jim.

Joe replied in a stupor,

"Hmmm?" he mumbled as he sat at the bar with his head in his hands, his matted brown hair heading in all directions out from under his fishing hat. You could not see his face, and that was a good thing.

This frustrated Jim even more.

Jim texted the others while waiting impatiently for Keene. There were responses, at least. Some had made it to the water and were heading out.

"Dammit, Joe, we are late!" yelled Jim. Joe didn't move with his head in his hands. "Wake up man, we have a tournament to win if you recall."

Joe lifted his head and his face was blood red and his eyes were even more so. He didn't say a word, but stood up and almost fell over. He reached for the bar and sat back down.

Oh my God, this is not going to go well, thought Jim.

Captain Keen finally came out with at least a bit of pep in his step. He was carrying a cup of coffee and a half gallon of Captain Morgan's.

"Time to shake it off chaps!" the captain said spritely. Joe heard that and came back to life, which was not much of a surprise to Jim. There was a reason they called him Drunk Joe.

Keene grabbed three shot glasses and started to pour the spiced rum.

"Hair of the Dog!" Joe chimed in with new life in his voice.

"Oh no!" yelled Jim. "Not me, and on that note I am out!. There is no way I am going on your ship of fools," Jim growled and did an about face, heading to the car. "You can go on Billy's boat without me."

He turned just in time to see the two toasting, and he almost threw up. When the empty shot glasses hit the bar, Captain Keene, Billy the Kid we called him, cleared his throat and chimed. "Oh, you are such a pansy, Jim. Just take a small swig and you will be fine."

There was no way in hell that Jim could imagine taking a sip of rum and getting on a boat. It was hard enough to control Drunk Joe as it was.

"Joe, I am going home and going back to bed. Come get the beer and your rods out of my car. And for that matter, you can take a cab home if Billy won't take ya."

Joe just looked at Jim with glazed eyes, then turned to Billy with a grimacing smile and poured another round. Jim's gag reflexes kicked in again, and he almost hurled. That was the last straw. He was not going fishing today. He should have known that this was going to happen. Just being in the bar on a Friday night was enough proof it would turn out this way.

"Come on, Jim, we need you out there today. Who am I going to best now?" joked 'Billy the Kid' Keene. "Just one shot and you will be back in the game."

Jim was fuming mad and turned to leave. He had been awaiting this day so bad.

Just like the Holidays, he thought as he stormed back to his car, all red eyed and head banging. It always happened that Jim enjoyed the anticipation of the holidays and vacation more than the actual sacred days themselves. The night before always seemed to turn out like this. He jumped in his car and sat there for a moment, debating turning the key.

Anticipation, he pondered. Why do I do this to myself? He sat there recalling the night before his maiden trip to the Island with his newly acquired boat. He and Manny had hit the Coco bar and restaurant before their big trip the next day to camp on the island. As planned, they had anchored right inside the inlet and passed out after their bar fun. Of course, Jim, being the Captain, had not contemplated the fact that he could not sleep. Once anchored, he was all ears, even in that pre-vacation intoxicated mode. By 5AM, as the fishing boats were rolling out, he was wide awake. This particular vacation he was recalling was the ceremonial trip to The Island, and he was so excited that he got trashed at the bar before they were to leave the inlet into the Atlantic sharply at dawn.

Damnit, he thought, recalling how he felt that next morning. Manny had pleaded to him to just go out the inlet, anchor for 20 minutes and take a nap to get at least some rest before the maiden voyage. Thank God he did, because he was fine after that. With the cool ocean breeze blowing through the porthole into the cabin, he had awoken feeling brand new and off they went!

This day is not the same. Jim tried one last time to convince himself to remain steadfast. *They just had shots for breakfast!* Jim pounded the steering wheel, turned the key and hit the gas, burning rubber backwards out of the driveway, slammed it in gear and smoked the tires again and sped home, feeling worse than he had in a very long time.

By the time Jim got home, his wife and son were still asleep, and Jim did the same as well. He awoke a few hours later to eat something. He couldn't remember if he had even talked to his wife before crashing, but he must have, as she had a comforting breakfast waiting for him. He told her of the great let down and she consoled him. He knew he had made the right choice, but he was still deeply saddened by the way things had turned out on his first official fishing tournament. In all reality, he knew it wasn't really official. All the entries were friends of friends from the local watering hole and by no means were they all professional or even dedicated enough to NOT get trashed the night before a big fishing event! He was still feeling that dark, sullen feeling of remorse. He ate and went back to bed, thanking his wife for putting up with him and his adventure seeking pirate friends. She understood. After all, it was the time of year when Spring Break was in full force and everyone was all about getting back to some major fun in the sun!

A few hours passed and Jim rolled over to find his wife shaking him. He was just starting to feel like himself again after some much needed food and shut-eye.

"Honey, your phone has been blowing up for the past hour. Billy has called at least ten times. Maybe they are in trouble," she whispered.

Jim rubbed his eyes and looked over at the clock. *It was 3PM already! Wow, that place was really rockin' last night,* he thought. Then suddenly he remembered; the tournament! He jumped out of bed and went downstairs to get his phone. Indeed, there were many missed calls and a voicemail from Billy. He listened to it, but it was all broken up and staticky. He immediately called him. No answer. He went to the kitchen to get a glass of water. Man, what a night and, more specifically, a morning.

It was still a blur. He was almost finished with his water and trying to recall the crazy ordeal, and the phone rang. It was Billy.

"What's up Billy? You guys alive out there, or did you even go?" he asked sarcastically.

"Of course we went and we are on our way back. Can you meet us at the dock? We have a bit of a problem," said Billy with a peculiar tone in his voice.

"What is it, man? Who do I need to take to the hospital.?" Jim said. He was sure he was being asked to help them with some tragic drunken mishap.

“No man, no time for your badgering. We are running on one engine at about 8 knots. We are 12 miles out. Jamaica Bob jumped in and was cooling off and somehow let the anchor fall. When we took off, it came from under the boat and wrapped around the starboard prop, and that engine is dead. Jim, we have the winning fish, the biggest Mahi I have ever caught! We will barely make it to the dock in time to drive it in. We need you to meet us there and run in our trophy fish. We may make it, but it will be close!”

Jim was in shock and fully awake now.

“Uh, ok, uh I am getting in the car now.” Jim quickly did the math as he ran outside. “It takes 20 minutes to get to the dock and another 25 to get to the bar. How long will it take you to get to the dock?” Jim asked. There was a moment of silence. Jim panicked.

“Keene, are you there? He paused. Keene?” The phone went dead. Jim kissed his wife, ran outside, jumped in the car, and cranked it up.

“At least no one drowned or was hurt,” he said to himself. Part of him wished he would have gone. “I guess there is a reason I stayed home today.”

The phone rang again as Jim pulled out of his driveway.

“Jim, you there?” came the voice of Captain Keene. Jim grunted as he barreled out of his subdivision.

I better drive safe. It will do no one any good if I get pulled over, he thought, his palms already sweating.

“I’m on the way, Bill. How far out are you?”

“I am about 7 miles out. I will make it there around 4:40. That will leave you about 15 minutes to get there. It will be a close, but you can make it. And Jim, we also have another problem.” Bill’s voice came all staticky and broken. It was a miracle he even had reception that far out.

“What is it Bill,” Jim asked. There was silence again. “Bill? Bill, can you hear me? I will be at the dock. Can you hear me?”

Jim hung up the phone and sped towards the dock. It was going to be a miracle if he could get the fish to the bar in time to weight it in.

Jim’s mind went wild, wondering what was the other problem. Maybe someone had drowned. Maybe there was an injury. He would know soon enough.

Jim was close to the dock now, his palms sweaty and adrenalin rushing through his body. He had gotten enough sleep. Not being a heavy drinker, he felt fine. Of all times for the bar to be in full swing. He recalled singing several of his favorite songs and chuckled in pride, thinking of their group rendition of Long Train Running by the Doobie Brothers. He loved to play his harmonica to that piece and last night they had really brought down the house! He could only imagine the agony he would have endured being out on the boat with those crazy pirate-like drunks.

As he pulled into the boat launch area, he saw the boat cruising up to the dock, several of the crew members on the bow holding the lines and ready to tie it up. They were scrambling all over the deck. He could see red in their faces. It must have been brutally hot out there.

He pulled straight up to the launch ramp, swung the car around and backed it up, leaving the car running. It was 23 minutes ‘til 5pm. There was no exception for the weigh-in cutoff time. He had to be quick. He ran down the dock screaming to hand over the fish. He could hear the Captain yelling out orders to the scurrying crew.

Before the lines were even secure and the boat snug against the dock, Jim saw the Keene take a running jump to the dock, almost missing it, catching himself and making his way to the car.

He was in terrible shape and looked exhausted, but he had a lustful look in his eyes.

"Ok, you and I are bringing in the prize Mahi. Bob and crew will pull the boat and meet us there," said the Billy, exasperated.

"Get me the fish, man. We are barely going to make it. We have twenty minutes and it takes twenty-five," Jim commanded.

The back door flew open and two people jumped into the back seat.

"Get out and get the fish in the trunk, now!" Jim screamed. Captain Keene repeated the same in support of Jim, who had come to the rescue.

"Get out and get that fish in the car", Keene repeated. "Jim and I will run the fish in, but we will be close!" There was pleading and drunken debating from the back seat, mainly from Drunk Joe.

"Out! Now" barked Billy.

Jim popped the trunk, the guys got out of the back seat and as soon as the trunk slammed shut, Jim hit the gas.

"Dammit, man, I didn't get to see the prize!" exclaimed Jim.

"Trust me, it is the winning fish. Now just focus on driving and do not get us killed or pulled over." pleaded Billy.

Jim did just that. He wildly got back on the Federal Highway and barreled down the road, bee-lining for the Rocky Bottom bar. He quickly veered over to Dixie Highway, taking a right onto 1st Avenue where the Captain had, only a few blocks over, been just hours ago enjoying the nightlife. The car almost lost traction, and he caught the back tires, locking them back in before careening into a bicycler on his morning spin.

“Easy Killer,” warned Billy. “We want to make it there alive and on time. It would be a sad ending to the day if you kill us both or a pedestrian.”

“Shut up,” growled Jim with white knuckles on the steering wheel. He looked at the clock below the dash and it showed five minutes ‘til five. It was going to be close.

Jim dared not say another word and kept focused on the road. He wanted to give Billy a piece of his mind, but he knew that was the past now and he needed to focus. They both remained tight-lipped. Billy had both hands on the dash. They could see the bar about a mile on the left. They were so close. The clock showed two minutes to five.

Just then a car, probably some old snow bird, pulled onto Dixie Highway less than a quarter of a mile ahead, taking its sweet beachcomber time. Another car was heading their way in the opposite lane. This would make or break them, thought Jim as he gunned it.

“Oh, shoot,” screamed Billy, as Jim left his lane and dared the oncoming car to a game of chicken. “Oh, shoot” Billy yelled again as Jim quickly cut in front of the slow car, barely making it back into his lane before careening the oncoming car. They heard a car horn changing pitch as they sped on. Jim looked over at Billy, who was white faced by now.

The bar was about 500 yards away. The clock showed 4:59. Jim didn’t slow down as he careened into the parking lot, hitting the emergency brake and skidded to a stop at the back entrance to the bar. Without a word, the two got out, grabbed the cooler and came running into the back entrance to the bar with the cooler, screaming, “Wait!”

The patron’s, all alarmed by the chaos, turned and stared.

The bar owner, Miguel, stepped up. Ok guys, relax, you made it. Let's get that leaky fish cooler out of my bar and out back to the scales.

Jim and Billy were still in shock. They had made it!

"Now show me that fish, Billy!" Jim exclaimed, still catching his breath. The cooler was not all the way shut. Jim could see a huge tail revealing itself from the closed lid. All the other contestants gathered around with much anxiety that they may not have won the tournament.

Miguel opened the cooler and stuffed inside was the biggest Bull Mahi Mahi that Jim had ever seen!

"It looks great," commented Captain Veroni, "but can it beat my 48 pound Mahi that is *my* winning fish?" It was going to be close.

There was a dead silence as Miguel hooked the tail of Billy's grand fish and lifted it onto the scale.

"We have our winner, weighing in at 53 pounds!" cried Miguel.

Billy and Jim looked at each other, still reeling from all the excitement, latched on to each other and started hugging and jumping around screaming.

"We won, Jim! Thank God you didn't go today!"

Jim continued bouncing around, then laughed. "I want my gas money back, Billy, and a big piece of the bounty for my grill!"

Billy, almost teary-eyed, replied almost immediately, "Sure thing Jim, ole buddy! Oh yeah, and the other bad news I was going to tell ya."

"Yes, what else?" Jim couldn't care less by now.

"Well, when we hooked the big catch, your lucky pirate's tumbler that you keep on my boat flew off the boat and was lost at sea."

"Jim hesitated and everyone waited for his response in silence."

"I won't be needing that anymore, replied Jim. After today, I quit drinking." The whole lot of folks at the Rocky Bottom bar started hee-hawing.

"Yeah, just like you will never sing karaoke again," retorted Billy the Kid, Keene.

You could hear the cheers and laughter as Jimmy Buffett's song, Margaritaville, played in the background, a fitting ending to another perilous adventure in South Florida!

About the Member Authors

Sharon Wynns: Sharon is a writer, artist and poet - an observer of human nature, a student of the human spirit and a disciple of Nature. Her second novel "Where Do We Go From Here" is in for publication with released scheduled for November 2021. She is working on her third, a sequel yet to be titled. Sharon says, "I write because it's so much fun! Sometimes, when I emerge from the story I am telling, my spirit is supercharged and I know I've been in touch with the magical source of creativity.

Rhonda Trueman: Originally from Charlotte, NC, is a new resident of Lavonia, GA. As an academic librarian, Rhonda published several professional articles and book chapters, but always yearned to write creative fiction. While living in Florida, Rhonda belonged to a poetry group, the Panhandle Poets Society and a folk music collaboration, the Pelican Pickers. Through these groups she found support and encouragement and is very excited to be a new member of the Bowers House Writers Guild. Now retired, Rhonda and her husband enjoy meeting others in the community and discovering everything this beautiful area has to offer. Georgia feels like home.

Robert Vasvary: Robert is a highly skilled engineer who has not given up on his desire to retire as a successful author. A true romantic, his stories and poems are layered with adventure, nostalgia, horror, romance, and tenderness. He is the successful author of "The Big House"–a book for young adults written to inspire his son. All he wants is to write for his bread and butter!

Pam Baker: Pam is originally from Evansville, Indiana where she raised her three sons. She now calls Royston, Georgia her home and raises flowers, vegetables, and chickens. Pam's early writing career consisted mostly of poetry, but since joining the Writer's Guild has discovered that she enjoys writing short stories just as much. She likes to blend fantasy with a little of her own life experience into each of her stories, which makes it even more fun to write. Pam published her first children's book, "The Adventures of Petey", recently and is currently working on its sequel.

Maxine Cobb: Maxine lives in Canon, Georgia. She discovered her interest in writing when she was introduced to the Writers Guild by her daughter. She has quickly built on her skills as a writer and storyteller. "I write to keep my memories fresh. Someday, my grandchildren may wonder about my life and times, perhaps they will learn about it through what I write.

I enjoy the fellowship at the Guild, the challenge of writing and learning to tell my stories better."

Linda H. Dye: Linda is a life-long resident of Elberton, Georgia. Linda published her first book "Of Our Times" in November 2020. It's a wonderful collection of stories subtitled: *A melding of memories and imaginings*. Linda says, "I have a rich full life. My interests are varied and I am always eager to try something new and exciting, meet a new person, travel to an unfamiliar place. My family and my church have been my focus over the years, but I am a voracious reader, a flower gardener, a watercolor painter, a Fun Club traveler, and, some say, a good cook. Writing is new to me; a delightful adventure in progress."

Carolyn Bond: Carolyn is a life-long resident of Elberton, Georgia. She writes local history stories for the Elberton Star. She recently published her first book, "Remember When…" based on the research coming out of these stories. Carolyn has a delightful, homespun storytelling style. Carolyn says, "I enjoy expressing my feelings. Telling the stories that lie within my heart means a lot to me. My writing helps those who know me, but never see me in the situations I write about, truly understand how I feel about life and history."

Bonnie McAlarney: Bonnie's first book "Memoirs, Musings and Morsels" tells stories about familiar people, places and events in her life that create a tapestry of a life beautifully lived. Books, words and creative thought fill her life. Her narrative style is rich, entertaining and woven with significant, thought-provoking meaning.

Ann Davis: Ann spent her adult life working with her husband in their greenhouse business, as well as rearing their two children. With retirement came time to pursue other interests. She joined The Writers Guild with no experience in writing, but a love for reading and the influence books have had in her life. Ann is known for her humorous prose but has a knack for producing mystery and drama as well. Ann says, "The enthusiasm and encouragement from other members have given me the incentive to write, rewrite, edit and try again."

Amanda Cantrell: Amanda is the daughter of Maxine Cobb. Photography and her dog are her special loves. Amanda says, "I write because I can't not write and have written stories and journaled all my life. I love taking thoughts in my head and putting them into words on paper so others can enjoy them. Writing is the sharing of the soul."

Elsa V. Salazar Krauss: Elsa is originally from Colombia, South America and she as been living in the United States for 52 years. She is a new member of the Bowers House Vriters Guild with no experience in writing but with a love for reading and a dream of someday riting her own Memoir. Elsa has had an interesting life backpacking, hiking, traveling, running riathlons and exploring caves. As an Environmental Engineer and a Chemist, Elsa enjoyed her vork outdoors, especially the 17 years she worked in the Florida Everglades. Having been lived a a farm, Elsa acquired a love for nature so her plans, as she is retired now, is to write about her ew adventures.